"Don't!"

She snatched her hand away from under his, clutching it firmly in her lap with her other hand.

He searched her face with thoughtful eyes. "What's wrong, Angelina? Are you still angry with me for what happened sixteen years ago? I wouldn't blame you if you were. I was thinking earlier today how much I wanted to say sorry to you for how things turned out that night, so if it's not too late, I'm truly sorry."

"No need for an apology." She bit out the words. "I was as much to blame as you were."

"Then what's the problem? Why snatch your hand away like that?"

Angelina could hardly tell him the truth. That just the touch of his hand fired up her hormones as no man had in the past sixteen years. Not even close. Even now she was looking at his mouth and wondering what it would feel like on hers again; wondering what making love would be like with Jake, now that he was older and much more experienced.

THE AUSTRALIANS

Where spirited women win the hearts of
Australia's most eligible men!

Experience the romance of Australia,
as only the bestselling authors from
Harlequin Presents® can imagine.

Coming soon to a store near you.

There's another Miranda Lee title
available in September:

The Magnate's Mistress
#2415

*Australian hotel magnate Max Richmond
was quite happy to keep Tara as his mistress—
but as the mother of his child…?*

Miranda Lee

THE PASSION PRICE

THE AUSTRALIANS

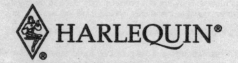

HARLEQUIN®

TORONTO • NEW YORK • LONDON
AMSTERDAM • PARIS • SYDNEY • HAMBURG
STOCKHOLM • ATHENS • TOKYO • MILAN • MADRID
PRAGUE • WARSAW • BUDAPEST • AUCKLAND

ISBN 0-373-12398-1

THE PASSION PRICE

First North American Publication 2004.

This edition published by arrangement with Harlequin Books S.A.

® and TM are trademarks of the publisher. Trademarks indicated with
® are registered in the United States Patent and Trademark Office, the
Canadian Trade Marks Office and in other countries.

www.eHarlequin.com

Printed in U.S.A.

CHAPTER ONE

'THE ad says the property is open for inspection every Saturday afternoon between two and three,' Dorothy pointed out. 'I'm going to drive up there today and have a look at it. What do you think of that?'

Jake put down the newspaper and looked up at the woman who'd been more of a mother to him than the woman who'd given birth to him thirty-four years before.

As much as he loved Dorothy, Jake wasn't going to indulge her in such a ridiculous idea.

'I think you're stark, raving mad,' he said.

Dorothy laughed, something she hadn't done all that often this past year.

Jake frowned. Maybe it wasn't such a ridiculous idea, if it made her happy.

Hell, no, he immediately reassessed. She was seventy-one years old. Way too old to go buying some run-down boutique winery up in the back blocks of the Hunter Valley.

Still, perhaps it would be wise not to mention Dorothy's age in his arguments. She was sensitive about that, like most women.

Not that she looked her age. Dorothy Landsdale was one of those women who had never been pretty,

5

but had grown more handsome with age. Tall, with broad shoulders and an impressive bosom, she had an intelligent face, with few lines on her perfect skin, a patrician nose and intense, deeply set blue eyes. Her silvery hair, which was dead straight, was always cut very short in a simple yet elegant style.

That was Dorothy's style all round. Simple, yet elegant. Jake had always admired the way she looked and dressed, although he sometimes wondered if she'd had her lips permanently painted red, because he'd never seen her without her favourite lipstick on.

Not that it mattered. Frankly, red lips suited her, especially when she was smiling.

Jake determined not to say anything that would wipe that wonderful smile off her face.

'Look, let's be sensible here,' he began in the same calm, cool, you-and-I-are-reasonable-people voice he reserved for juries during his closing addresses. 'You know nothing about wine-making.'

'Actually, you're wrong there, Jake, dear. You obviously don't know this, but Edward once planned on buying a boutique winery in the Hunter Valley. He fancied going up there on weekends. He collected a whole shelf-full of books on the subject of wine and wine-making at the time. Made me read them so we could talk about the subject together. But then he brought you home to live with us and that idea was abandoned. Though never entirely forgotten. He still dreamt of doing it after he retired.'

Jake experienced a dive in spirits, as he always did when the judge was talked about. He and Dorothy had both been shattered when Dorothy's husband of thirty years had died of a coronary last year, a few short months before his retirement. Jake had taken the news extra hard. If Dorothy was like a mother to him, Edward had been like a father, and more. He'd been Jake's mentor and best friend. His saviour, in fact. A wonderful man. Kind and generous and truly wise.

Jake knew he would never meet his like again.

Edward had left Jake a small fortune in his will, an astonishing document with a written request that within six months of his death Jake was to use some of his cash legacy to buy a luxury harbourside apartment and a yellow Ferrari. Jake had wept when he'd been told this. He'd confided these two fantasy purchases to his friend one night last year over a game of chess, also confessing that he would probably never buy them, even if he could afford to. He already had a perfectly nice apartment, he had explained to Edward. And a reliable car.

But Edward's last wishes were sacrosanct with Jake and he'd taken possession of the new apartment—set on prestigious McMahon's Point—just before Christmas a couple of months back. The Ferrari had come only last week. He'd had to wait ages to have a yellow one imported and delivered.

Both the apartment and the car had already given him great pleasure. But he would give them both back—hell, he'd practically sell his soul to the devil—to have the man himself sitting alive and well at this breakfast table with them.

'So that's what this is all about,' he said with a raw edge in his voice. 'You want to make Edward's dream come true.'

'In a way. But don't get me wrong. This would mostly be for me. I need a new venture, Jake. A new interest in life. Edward would hate for me to be moping around all the time, thinking my life was over because he was no longer here. When I saw that ad in the *Herald* this morning, it jumped right out at me. But it's not just the winery. I simply love the look of the house.'

Jake glanced down at the photograph of the house. 'It just looks old to me.'

'It's beautiful. I love old Australian farmhouses. Look at those gorgeous wraparound verandas. First thing I'd buy would be a swing seat. I'd sit there every afternoon with a gin and tonic and watch the sunsets. I've never had a house, you know. I've always lived in apartments. I've never had a garden, either.'

'They're a lot of work, houses and gardens,' Jake pointed out. 'Wineries, too,' he added, suddenly thinking of another time and another winery.

It, too, had been in the Hunter Valley. But not one of the boutique varieties. A reasonably large winery with acres under vine, producing tons of grapes each season that the anti-machinery Italian owner always had picked by hand.

Which was where he had come in.

Jake hadn't thought about that place, or that time

in his life, for ages. He'd trained himself over the years not to dwell on past miseries, or past mistakes.

But now that he had, the memories came swarming back. The heat that summer. The back-breaking work. And the utter boredom.

No wonder his eyes had kept going to the girl.

She'd been the only child of the Italian owner. Angelina, her name was. Angelina Mastroianni. Lush and lovely, with olive skin, jet-black hair, big brown eyes and a body that had looked fabulous in the short shorts and tight tank tops she lived in.

But it was her come-hither glances which he'd noticed the most.

As a randy and rebellious seventeen-year-old, Jake had been no stranger to sex. No stranger to having girls come on to him, either.

Yet it had taken him all summer to talk Angelina into meeting him alone. He'd thought she was playing hard to get, a conclusion seemingly backed up by the way she'd acted as soon as he'd drawn her into his arms. She hadn't been able to get enough of his kisses, or his hands. He hadn't discovered till after the big event, and her father was beating him to a pulp, that she'd only been fifteen, and a virgin to boot.

Within the hour, he'd been bundled off back to the teenage refuge in Sydney from whence he'd come. The subsequent charge of carnal knowledge had brought him up in front of the very man who'd sent him on the 'character-building' work programme at the winery in the first place.

Judge Edward Landsdale.

Jake had been scared stiff of actually being convicted and sentenced, something he'd miraculously managed to avoid during his rocky young life so far. But he'd felt his luck had run out on this occasion and the prospect of a stint in an adult jail loomed large in his mind, given that he was almost eighteen.

Fear had made him extra-belligerent, and even more loud-mouthed than usual. Judge Landsdale had seen right through him, and also seen something else. God bless him. Somehow, Edward had had the charges dropped, and then he'd done something else, something truly remarkable. He'd brought Jake home to live with him and his wife.

That had been the beginning of Jake's new life, a life where he realised there were some good people in this world, and that you could make something of yourself, if someone had faith in you and gave you very real, hands-on support.

Angelina had lingered in Jake's thoughts for a long time after that fateful night. In the end, however, he'd forced her out of his mind and moved on, filling his life with his studies and, yes, other girls.

Now that he came to think of it, however, none of his girlfriends so far had ever made him feel what Angelina had made him feel that long-ago summer.

Who knew why that was? Up till their rendezvous in the barn, they'd only talked. Perhaps it had been the long, frustrating wait which had made even kissing her seem so fabulous. The sex had hardly been memorable. She'd panicked at the last moment and he'd had to promise to pull out. Then, when she'd been so tight, he hadn't twigged why—young fool that he was. His only excuse was that he'd been totally carried away at the time.

Really, the whole thing had been nothing short of a fiasco, with her father finding them together in the winery only seconds after Jake had done the dastardly deed. He'd barely had time to zip his jeans up before the first blow connected with his nose, breaking it and spurting blood all over one highly hysterical Angelina.

Jake reached up to slowly rub the bridge of his nose.

It wasn't crooked any longer. Neither were his front teeth still broken. He didn't have any tattoos left, either. Dorothy had taken him to the best Macquarie Street cosmetic surgeons and dentists within weeks of his coming to live with her, beginning his transformation from Jake Winters, dead-beat street kid and born loser, to Jake Winters, top litigator and sure winner.

He wondered what had happened to Angelina in the intervening years. No doubt that hotheaded father of hers would have kept a closer eye on his precious daughter after that night. He'd had big dreams for his winery, had Antonio Mastroianni. Big dreams for his lovely Angelina as well.

With the wisdom of hindsight, Jake could now well understand the Italian's reaction to discovering them together. The last male on earth any father would have wanted his daughter to get tangled up with was the likes of himself. He'd been a bad boy back then. A very bad boy.

Not to Judge Edward Landsdale, though. When Edward had first met Jake, he hadn't seen the long hair, the tattoos or the countless body piercings. All he'd seen was a good boy crying to get out, a boy worth helping.

Aah, Edward. You were right, and wrong at the same time. Yes, I *have* made something of myself, thanks to you and Dorothy. But beneath my sophisticated and successful veneer, I'm still that same street kid. Tough and hard and self-centred in the way you had to become on Sydney's meaner streets to survive. Basically, a loner. Such programming is deep-seated, and possibly the reason why my personal life is not as great as my professional life.

A top trial lawyer might benefit from being on the cold-blooded side, from never letting emotion get in the way of his thinking. But how many of my girlfriends have complained of my lack of sensitivity? My selfishness? My inability to truly care about them, let alone commit?

I might be able to argue great cases and win verdicts, along with massive compensation payments for my clients, but I can't keep a woman in my life for longer than a couple of months.

And do I care?

Not enough.

The truth is I like living alone, especially now, in my fantastic harbourside apartment. I like being responsible for no one but myself.

Dorothy, of course, was a responsibility of sorts. But Dorothy was different. He loved Dorothy as much as he had loved Edward. That was why he visited her every Friday night, and why he sometimes stayed the night. To make sure she was all right. Edward would have wanted him to look after Dorothy, and he aimed to do just that.

Not an easy task, Jake reminded himself, if she was living way out in the country.

He really had to talk her out of the ridiculously romantic idea of buying this winery.

But talking Dorothy out of something was not always an easy thing to do...

When Jake's eyes glazed over and he kept idly rubbing his nose, Dorothy wondered what he was thinking about. Edward, probably. Poor Jake. Edward's death had really rocked him. They'd become so close over the years, those two. The crusty old judge with the heart of gold and the cocky street kid with no heart at all.

Till Jake had met Edward, that was.

Impossible to remain completely heartless around Edward. Dorothy knew that for a fact. The day she'd met her future husband, she'd been forty years old. Overweight and on the frumpy side, way past her prime. Edward had been five years younger at thirty-five, tall and handsome and beautifully dressed. He'd come to her aid when she'd been knocked over in Market Place by some lout on a skateboard. He'd taken her for a cup of coffee to settle her nerves and swiftly made her forget that she was a dried-up old spinster with a dreary office job and a bitter cynicism about men, especially the good-looking ones.

She'd fallen in love with Edward that very first day. Why he'd fallen in love with her, she had no idea. He'd claimed it was the heat in her eyes. Whatever, she'd lost those extra pounds she'd been carrying over the next few weeks. In her few spare hours, she'd also smartened herself up. Bought some decent clothes. Had her hair styled by a good hairdresser. And started always wearing the red lipstick Edward had admired.

They'd been married six months later, to predictions of doom from relatives. But their marriage had proved to be a great success, despite their not having any children.

Other men might have resented that. But not Edward. When she'd tearfully questioned him over his feelings about her infertility, he'd hugged her and said he'd married her for better or worse, and that resenting realities was a waste of time. But that was when he'd started working with charities that helped underprivileged boys, and where he'd lavished all his unused fatherly love.

Still, he hadn't become too personally involved with any of the boys till Jake had come along. Jake, of the ice-blue eyes and serious attitude problem.

When Edward had first brought Jake home to live with them, Dorothy couldn't stand the boy's smart mouth and slovenly ways. But gradually, a miracle had happened. Jake had changed and maybe she had changed a bit, too, becoming more tolerant and understanding.

Whatever, they'd both ended up genuinely liking each other. No, *loving* each other. Like mother and son.

Dorothy knew that if she bought this winery Jake would come and visit her up there as much as he did here, in Sydney. The Hunter Valley wasn't all that far away. A two-hour drive. It would do him good, she thought, to get out of the city occasionally. To relax and smell the flowers, so to speak. He worked way too hard. And it wasn't as though there was any special girl to keep him here in Sydney at the weekends. He'd broken up with that last one he'd been dating. A bottle-blonde with a flashy smile and a figure to match.

Why Jake kept choosing girls for their sex appeal alone, Dorothy couldn't fathom. When she'd complained about this side of Jake to Edward a couple of years back, he'd said not to worry. One day, Jake would meet the right girl, fall head over heels, get married and have a family.

Dorothy wasn't so sure about that last part. She didn't think having a family would ever be on Jake's agenda. Damaged children often veered away from having children themselves.

No, she wasn't holding her breath over that ever happening.

'Penny for your thoughts,' she said gently.

Jake snapped back to reality with a dry laugh.

'Not worth even ten cents. So when do you want to leave?'

Dorothy smiled. 'You're going to drive me up there?'

Jake shrugged. 'Can't let my best girl go careering all over the countryside by herself. Besides, I've been dying for an excuse to give my new car a proper spin. Can't do that on city roads.'

'Jake Winters! I have no intention of dying at the hands of some speed-happy fool in a yellow Ferrari.'

Jake laughed. 'And this from the wild woman who's planning to buy some run-down winery in the middle of nowhere! Don't worry, I won't go over the speed limit. And hopefully, once you see this dump for real, you'll be happy to stay right where you are and take up pottery.'

'Pottery! What a good idea! There's sure to be room for a kiln at the winery. The ad says there are ten acres of land, and only five under vine.'

Jake gave up at this point. But he was sure that Dorothy *would* see the folly of her ways and change her mind once she saw the place, and where it was.

'If we leave around ten,' Dorothy said excitedly, 'we'd get up there in time for lunch. Lots of the larger wineries have great restaurants, you know.'

Jake frowned. Mr Mastroianni had been going to build a restaurant at his winery. And guest accommodation. He'd also been going to change the name of the winery from its present unprepossessing name to something more exotic-sounding. Angelina had told him all about her *papa*'s grand plans, but Jake's mind had been on other things at the time and he couldn't remember what the new name was. Or what the old name was, for that matter. Though it hadn't been Italian.

According to Angelina, the winery had belonged to her mother's family. Jake did recall her telling him that her mother had been middle-aged when her father married her. She'd died having Angelina.

'I looked up a few of the restaurants on the internet last night,' Dorothy was rattling on. 'There's this really interesting-looking one on the same road as the place we're going to inspect. It's at a winery called the Ambrosia Estate. Isn't that a wonderful name for a winery? The nectar of the gods.'

Jake's mouth dropped open. That was it! *Ambrosia!*

'What is it?' Dorothy said. 'What did I say?'

'Did Edward ever tell you the story of how I came to be in his court?'

'Yes. Yes, of course. You...' She broke off, her eyes widening. 'Good lord, you don't mean...'

'Yep. The scene of my crime was the Ambrosia Estate.'

'Goodness! What an amazing coincidence!'

'My thoughts exactly.'

Dorothy gave him a sheepish look. 'I—er—I've already made us a booking at the restaurant there for twelve-thirty.'

Jake couldn't help being amused. What a crafty woman she was. 'You were very confident I'd drive you up there myself, weren't you?'

'I think I know you pretty well by now. But honestly, Jake, if you want me to change the booking to somewhere else, it's easily done.'

'No, don't worry. I doubt I'd be recognised. I've changed somewhat since my bad-boy days, don't you think? Though it's just as well *you* made the booking. If old-boy Mastroianni knew Jake Winters was eating lunch in his restaurant, I'd be fed hemlock. Italians have long memories and a penchant for revenge. He might not know my face but I'll bet he'd remember my name.'

Oh, yes. He'd bet the name Jake Winters was burned into Antonio Mastroianni's brain. And whilst Jake really didn't want another confrontation with Angelina's father, the possibility of running into Angelina again sparked an undeniable surge of excitement.

She would be what age now? Thirty-one? Thirty-two? Had to be thirty-two. She'd been two years younger than him and he was thirty-four.

Logic told Jake that a thirty-two-year-old Italian girl would be long married by now, with a brood of *bambinos* around her skirts.

At the same time he reasoned that even if she was married, she'd probably still be living at the winery, with her husband working in the family business. That was the way of Italians. No, she was sure to be there, somewhere.

The desire to see Angelina again increased. Was it

just curiosity, or the need to say he was sorry for what he'd done? She'd been terribly upset at the time.

But what would an apology achieve after all these years? What would be the point?

No point at all, Jake decided with a return to his usual pragmatism. Best he just have his lunch and leave. Maybe he'd catch a glimpse of Angelina. And maybe he wouldn't.

Who knew? He probably wouldn't recognise her. It was sixteen years ago after all.

CHAPTER TWO

'YOU can look for your father when you turn sixteen,' Angelina promised.

'But that's not till November!' her son protested. 'Why do I have to wait that long? It's not as though Grandpa's around any more to get upset. I mean…Oh, gosh, I know that sounded bad. Look, I miss Grandpa as much as you do, Mum. But this is important to me. I want to meet my dad. See what he looks like. *Talk* to him.'

'Has it occurred to you that he might not want to meet you? He doesn't even know you exist!'

'Yeah, I know that, but that's not his fault, is it? No one ever told him. He's got a right to know he has a son.'

Angelina sighed into the phone. She still could not come to terms with Alex's sudden obsession with finding his biological father. Every time she rang her son at school, and vice versa, it was his main topic of conversation.

Of course, when his grandfather had been alive, the subject of Jake Winters had been forbidden. In Antonio Mastroianni's eyes, the tattooed lout who'd seduced and impregnated his daughter was nothing better than a disgusting animal, not worthy of dis-

cussion. Alex's birth certificate said 'father un-
known'.

When Alex had been old enough to ask questions,
his grandfather had told him that his father had been
bad, and that he was lucky not to have anything to
do with him. He, Antonio Mastroianni, would be his
father as well as his grandfather. In return, Alex
would carry the Mastroianni name and inherit the
family estate.

To give her father credit, he had heaped a great
deal of love and attention on Alex. The boy had
adored his grandpa in return and, in accordance with
his grandfather's wishes, Alex's father was never
mentioned.

But within weeks of his grandfather's tragic death
late last year, Alex had started asking his mother
questions about his real father, wheedling Jake's
name out of her, then every other detail about him
that she could remember, before finally demanding
that they try to find him.

Just the thought of coming face to face with Jake
again after all these years had put Angelina into a
panic, which was why she'd initially come up with
the 'wait-till-you're-sixteen' idea. But since then,
she'd thought about the situation more calmly and
stuck to her guns.

Because heaven only knew what Jake, the grown
man, would be like. The last she'd heard he'd been
going to be charged with carnal knowledge and
would probably go to jail, something which had

given her nightmares at the time. Till another nightmare had consumed her thoughts, and her life.

At worst, Jake might now be a hardened criminal. At best, Angelina still doubted he'd be the kind of man she'd want her son to spend too much time around. She didn't agree with her father that Jake had been born bad. But maturity—and motherhood—made her see Jake in a different light these days. He *had* been from the wrong side of the tracks, a neglected and antisocial young man, something that time rarely fixed.

'I don't want to discuss this any further, Alex,' she stated unequivocally. 'That's my decision and I think it's a fair and sensible one.'

'No, it's not,' he grumbled.

'Yes, it is. By sixteen, hopefully you'll be old enough to handle whatever you find out about your father. Trust me. I doubt it will be good news. He's probably in jail somewhere.'

Silence from the other end.

Angelina hated having to say anything that might hurt her son, but why pretend? Crazy to let him weave some kind of fantasy about his father, only to one day come face to face with a more than sobering reality.

'You said he was smart,' Alex pointed out.

'He was.' Street-smart.

'And good-looking.'

'Yes. Very.' In that tall, dark and dangerous fashion that silly young girls were invariably attracted to. She'd found everything about Jake wildly exciting

back then, especially the symbols of his rebellious-
ness. He'd had studs in his ears, as well as his nose,
a ring through one nipple and a tattoo on each upper
arm. Lord knew how many other tattoos he'd have
by now.

'In that case, he's not in jail,' Alex pronounced
stubbornly. 'No way.'

Angelina rolled her eyes. 'That's to be seen in
November, isn't it? But for now I'd like you to settle
down and concentrate on your studies. You're doing
your school certificate this year.'

'Waste of time,' Alex growled. 'I should be at
home there with you, helping with the harvest and
making this year's wines. Grandpa always said that
it was crazy for people to go to university and do
degrees to learn how to make wine. Hands-on experience is the right way. He told me I'd already had
the best apprenticeship in the world, and that I was
going to be a famous wine-maker one day.'

'I fully agree with him. And I'd never ask you to
go to university and get a degree. I'm just asking you
to stay at school till you're eighteen. At the very
school, might I remind you, that your grandfather
picked out for you. He was adamant that you should
get a good education.'

'OK,' he replied grudgingly. 'I'll do it for
Grandpa. But the moment I finish up here, you're
getting rid of that old fool you've hired and I'm going to do the job I was brought up to do.'

'Arnold is not an old fool,' Angelina said. 'Your

grandfather said he was once one of the best wine-makers in the valley.'

'Once, like a hundred years ago?' her son scoffed.

'Arnold is only in his sixties.' Sixty-nine, to be exact.

'Yeah, well, he looks a hundred. I don't like him and I don't like him making our wines,' Alex stated firmly, and Angelina knew her son's mind would never be swayed on that opinion. He'd always been like that, voicing his likes and dislikes in unequivocal terms from the time he could talk. If he didn't like a certain food, he'd simply say, 'Don't like it.' Then close his mouth tightly.

No threat or punishment would make him eat that food.

Stubborn, that was what he was. Her father had used to say he got it from him. But Angelina suspected that trait had come from a different source, as did most of Alex's physical genes as well. His height, for one.

Alex had been taller than his grandfather at thirteen. At fifteen he was going on six feet, and still growing. And then there were his eyes. An icy blue they were, just like Jake's. With long lashes framing them. His Roman nose possibly belonged to the Mastroianni side, as well as his olive skin. But his mouth was pure Jake. Wide, with full lips, the bottom lip extra-full.

He'd probably end up a good kisser, just like his father.

'I have to go, Alex,' she said abruptly. 'I'm needed

up at the restaurant for lunch. It's always extra-busy on a Saturday when the weather's nice.'

'Yeah. OK. I have to go, too. Practise my batting. Kings School are coming over this afternoon to play cricket. We're going to whip their butts this time.'

Angelina smiled. For all her son's saying he wanted to be home at the winery, he really enjoyed life at his city boarding-school. He'd been somewhat lonely as an only child, living on a country property.

Located on Sydney's lower North Side, St Francis's College had come highly recommended, with a sensible balance of good, old-fashioned discipline and new-age thinking. Their curriculum included loads of sports and fun activities to keep their male students' hormones and energy levels under control.

This was Alex's fourth year there and he was doing very well, both in the classroom and on the sports field. He played cricket in summer and soccer in winter, but swimming was his favourite sport. The shelves in his bedroom were chock-full of swimming trophies.

'Good luck, then,' Angelina said. 'I'll give you a ring after you've whipped their butts. Now I really must go, love. *Ciao.*'

She hung up, then frowned. Cricket might distract Alex from his quest to find his father for the moment, but she didn't like her chances of putting her son off till his birthday in November. That was nine long months away.

Nine months…

Angelina's chest contracted at the thought that it was around this time sixteen years ago that she'd conceived. Late February. Alex's birthday was the twenty-fourth of November.

Today was the twenty-fourth, she realised with a jolt. And a Saturday as well. The anniversary of what had been the most earth-shattering day of her life.

Angelina shook her head as she sank down on the side of her bed, her thoughts continuing to churn away. She did not regret having Alex. She loved him more than anything in the world. He'd given her great joy.

But there'd been great misery to begin with. Misery and anguish. No one could understand what it had been like for her. She'd felt so alone, without a mother to comfort her, and with a father who'd condemned her.

Antonio Mastroianni hadn't come round till the day Alex had been born, the day he'd held Angelina's hand through all the pain of childbirth and finally realised she wasn't just a daughter who'd disappointed him, but a living, breathing human being who was going through a hell of her own.

After that, things had been better between them, but nothing would change the fact that she'd become a single mother at the tender age of sixteen. By the time Alex had been born, she'd long left school, plus lost all her school friends. When she'd come home from the hospital, there had just been herself in the house all day with a crying, colicky baby and her father, who tried to help, but was pretty useless.

Some days she'd wanted to scream at the top of her lungs. Instead, often, she'd just sat down and cried along with Alex.

Meeting Jake Winters that summer sixteen years ago had sure changed her life forever. And the thought of meeting him again scared the living daylights out of her.

Not because she felt in danger of falling in love with him again. Such an idea was ludicrous. But because of the danger of Alex falling under his father's possibly bad influence. She hadn't sacrificed her whole life to raise a secure, stable, happy boy, only to surrender him to someone she didn't really know, and possibly couldn't trust. Alex needed good male role models now that his grandfather wasn't around to direct him, not some rebel-without-a-cause type.

Angelina tried to imagine what Jake would be like today. Could he possibly have come good, or had he gone down the road to self-destruction? Was he even alive? Maybe she should start looking for him herself, do a preliminary reconnoitre. She didn't have to hire anybody, not to begin with. She could ring all the J Winters in the Sydney phone book first.

Yes, that was what she would do. She'd get on to that tomorrow. She would try in the evening. Most people were home on a Sunday evening.

Another thought suddenly popped into her mind.

What if he was married, with a wife and a family?

Angelina knew the answer to that as surely and instinctively as Alex had known that his father was not in jail.

No way!

The Jake who'd chatted her up that summer had been a hater of all things traditional and conservative. Marriage would never be for him. Or family life. Or even falling in love. She'd grown up sufficiently now to see that Jake hadn't cared about her one bit back then. All their intimate conversations whilst grape-picking together had been nothing but a way for him to get into her pants.

Which he had. But only the once. And even that must have been an anticlimax, for want of a better word.

Looking back, it was ironic that she hadn't enjoyed the actual event that had ruined her life at the time. She might have borne the memory better if she'd been carried away on the wings of ecstasy to the very end.

Jake's lovemaking had promised well to begin with. He'd been more than a good kisser, actually. He was a *great* kisser. His hands had been just as effective, with a built-in road map to all her pleasure zones. Her breasts. Her nipples. And of course the white-hot area between her legs. Soon she'd been all for him going all the way, despite some last-minute panic over getting pregnant. But the sharp pain she experienced when he penetrated her had swiftly brought her back to earth. All she'd felt during the next ten seconds or so was a crushing wave of disappointment.

Even if her father hadn't watched over her after Jake like a hawk, Angelina had steadfastly refused to become one of those single mums whose son woke up to a different man in his mummy's bed every other week. She'd made her bed, as her father had often told her, and she'd bravely resolved to lie in it. Alone.

To be honest, however, her opportunities for having even a brief fling hadn't exactly been thick on the ground to begin with. As the stay-home mother of a young child, she'd rarely been in the company of eligible men. Her weekly shopping trip to the nearby town of Cessnock had been her only regular outing. In fact, Angelina hadn't been asked out by a single member of the opposite sex till three years ago.

Two things had happened around that time to greatly change her life circumstances. Alex had gone off to boarding school and she'd enrolled in a computer course at the local technical college. She'd known she had to do something to fill the great hole in her life created by her precious son going off to school.

Once she had some computer skills under her belt, Angelina had felt confident enough to try working on the reception desk at the resort. To her surprise, she'd taken to the service industry like a duck to water. Soon, she'd been also escorting groups of guests on tours of the property, serving in the cellar and helping out at the restaurant at lunchtime on the weekends, its busiest time. She just loved talking to people, and they seemed to like talking to her.

Before this, she'd only done behind-the-scenes

jobs around the resort such as cooking and cleaning, hardly esteem-building activities. Not that she'd had much self-esteem by then. Her stay-at-home years when Alex had been a baby and a toddler had gradually eroded her confidence and turned her from an outgoing girl into a reserved, almost shy woman.

Now, suddenly, she had blossomed again, thoroughly enjoying the social interaction and yes, the admiration—however meaningless and fleeting—of the opposite sex.

She'd begun taking care with her appearance again, exercising off some of the extra pounds which had crept on over the years and paying more attention to her hair, her clothes and her make-up.

Of course, her father had noticed her transformation, plus the attention of the male tourists and guests. And yes, of course, he'd commented and criticised. But this time she'd put him firmly in his place, telling him she was a grown woman and he was to keep out of her personal and private life.

Not that there'd been one. Despite her father suspecting otherwise, she *hadn't* taken up any of the none too subtle offers she'd received from the many men who now asked her out. She didn't even want to go out with them, let alone go to bed with them. Maybe it was crazy to use her teenage experience with Jake as a basis for comparison, but none of these men had made her feel even a fraction of what she'd felt when she first met Jake.

Of course, Angelina understood that the intensity of her feelings for Jake had largely been because of her age. He'd represented everything that a young, virginal girl found wildly exciting.

Angelina had no doubt that if Jake himself walked back into her life at this moment, she would not feel anything like she had back then. She no longer found long-haired, tattooed males even remotely attractive, for starters. The sight of him might make her heart race, but only with fear, fear of the bad influence he might have on her highly impressionable and very vulnerable son.

Thinking of this reminded her that, sooner or later, she *would* come face to face with Alex's father again, possibly sooner rather than later, if she started those phone calls tomorrow evening.

The thought bothered her a great deal.

'Damn you, Jake,' she muttered as she stood up and marched across her bedroom towards her *en suite* bathroom. 'Sixteen years, and you're still causing me trouble!'

CHAPTER THREE

THE yellow Ferrari caught Angelina's eye the moment it turned from the main road into the Ambrosia Estate. She stopped what she was doing—opening a bottle of wine at one of the outdoor tables—and watched the brightly coloured sports car crunch to a halt in the nearby car park, her lips pursing into a silent whistle when a dark-haired hunk in designer jeans, pale blue polo shirt and wraparound sunglasses climbed out from behind the wheel.

What a gorgeous-looking guy!

Angelina's gaze shifted over to the passenger side. She could see another person sitting in the car but couldn't make out any details. The sun was shining on the windscreen. But Angelina was willing to bet on it being a pretty blonde. Men like that invariably had pretty blondes on their arms.

The hunk hitched his jeans up onto his hips as hunks often did. Not because his clothes really needed straightening, she'd come to realise during her recent people-watching years. It was a subconscious body-language thing, a ploy to draw female attention to that part of his body.

And it worked. Angelina certainly looked, as did the two middle-aged ladies she was serving. Both widows, their names were Judith and Vivien. They were on holiday together and had been staying at the Ambrosia Estate for a few days.

'Cocky devil,' Judith said with a wry smile in her voice when the hunk started striding round the front of the yellow Ferrari in the direction of the passenger side.

'He has every right to be,' Vivien remarked. 'Just look at that car.'

Judith snorted. 'Don't you mean, just look at that body?'

Angelina had actually stopped looking at the hunk's broad-shouldered, slim-hipped, long-legged body and was frowning over his walk. It was a most distinctive walk, somewhere between a strut and a swagger. He moved as if he was bouncing along on the balls of his feet.

'Jake…'

The word escaped her lips before she could help it, and her two lady customers immediately looked up at her.

'You *know* the guy with the yellow sports car?' Judith asked, grey eyes narrowed. She was the sharper of the two ladies.

'No,' Angelina denied, dismissing the crazy notion that the man could possibly be Jake. 'But his walk reminded me of someone I used to know.'

'A sexy someone, I'll bet.'

Angelina had to smile. 'Very.' She pulled out the cork on the bottle of chilled Verdelho and poured both ladies a full glass. Each one immediately lifted their glass to their lips. They did like their wine, those two.

The emergence of a grey-haired lady from the passenger seat of the Ferrari surprised the three of them.

'Good lord!' Judith exclaimed. 'Not quite what I was expecting. So what do you reckon, girls? His mother? Or do we cast lover boy in the role of gigolo?'

'Oh, surely not,' Vivien said with a delicate little shudder.

'You're right,' Judith went on. 'She's much too old to be bothered with that kind of thing. But she's not his mother, either. Too old for that as well. Possibly a great-aunt. Or a client. He might be her financial adviser. She looks as rich as he does.'

'I'll leave you two ladies to speculate,' Angelina said as she placed the bottle in the portable wine cooler by their table. 'Wilomena will be over shortly to take your orders. Enjoy your meal.' And your gossiping, she added silently.

As she made her way back inside, Angelina threw another glimpse over her shoulder at the man and woman who were now walking together along the path that led over the small footbridge, past the outdoor dining area and along to the main door of the restaurant. The hunk was holding the woman's arm but his head was moving from side to side as though he was looking for something. Or someone.

Angelina found herself hurrying out of his line of sight, tension gripping her insides. Her actions—plus her sudden anxiety—really irritated her. As if it could possibly be Jake! How fanciful could she get?

That's what you get when you start thinking about ghosts from the past, Angelina. You conjure one up!

She resisted the temptation to watch the hunk's approach through the picture-glass windows of the restaurant, though she did go straight to the counter where they kept the reservation book, her eyes dropping to run over the names that had been booked for lunch. There was no Winters amongst them.

Of course not. Why would there be? The hunk just walked like Jake, that was all. OK, so he *was* built a bit like Jake as well. *And* he had similar-coloured hair.

Dark brown hair, however, was hardly unusual. On top of that, this guy's hair was cropped very short, almost in a military style. Jake had been proud of his long hair. He would never have it cut like that. Not that the short-all-over look didn't suit the hunk. It was very…macho.

Jake had been very macho.

It couldn't be him, could it?

Once he came inside and took off those sunglasses, Angelina reassured herself, there would no longer be any doubt in her mind.

And if he *did* have eyes like chips of blue ice? came the gut-tightening question. What then? How did you deal with such an appalling coincidence? What sick fate would send him back to her today, of all days?

The restaurant door opened and Angelina forced

herself to look up from where she was practically hiding behind the front counter.

The hunk propped the door open with one elbow and ushered his elderly companion in ahead of him. The lady was not so fragile-looking up close, her face unlined and her blue eyes bright with good health. But she had to be seventy, if she was a day.

And the hunk? It was impossible to tell his age till he took those darned sunglasses off. He could have been anywhere between twenty-five and forty, although there was an air of self-assurance about him that suggested he'd been around a while.

The grey-haired lady stepped up to the counter first. 'I made a booking for two for twelve-thirty,' she said with a sweet smile. 'The name's Landsdale. Mrs Landsdale.'

Angelina was highly conscious of the hunk standing at the lady's shoulder. Was he staring at her from behind those opaque shades? It felt as if he was.

'Yes, I have your booking here, Mrs Landsdale,' she replied, proud of herself for sounding so polite and professional in the face of the tension that was building inside her. 'Would you like to dine inside, or alfresco? It's really lovely outside today. No wind. Not too hot. And not too many flies.'

The lady's smile widened. 'Alfresco sounds wonderful. What do you think, Jake? Shall we sit outside?'

Angelina froze. Had she heard correctly? Had the woman really said that name?

Angelina stared, open-mouthed, as he finally took

off his sunglasses, her whole world tipping on its axis.

It *was* him. Those eyes could not possibly belong to anyone else.

'Jake,' she blurted out whilst her head whirled with the incredibility of this scenario.

'Hello, Angelina,' he said in the same richly masculine voice he'd already had at seventeen. 'I'm surprised you recognised me after all these years.'

If it hadn't been for the eyes, she might not have. He was *nothing* like the boy she remembered, or the man she'd imagined he might have become. This Jake was smooth and suave and sophisticated. More handsome than ever and obviously no longer underprivileged.

'Goodness, you mean *this* is Angelina,' the grey-haired lady piped up before Angelina could find a suitable reply. 'Jake, you naughty boy. Why didn't you say something earlier?'

He lifted his broad shoulders in an elegant shrug. 'I spotted her through the windows, and decided if she didn't recognise me back I wouldn't embarrass her by saying anything.'

Well, at least that meant he hadn't deliberately come looking for her, Angelina realised with some relief. Still, this was an amazing coincidence, given she'd been thinking about him all morning. She could feel herself trembling inside with shock.

'I—er—didn't recognise you till you took off your sunglasses,' she admitted whilst she struggled to pull herself together. *Think,* girl.

'You do have very distinctive eyes, Jake,' she added, bracing herself to look into them once more. This time she managed without that ridiculous jolt to her heart.

'Do I?' he said with a light laugh. 'They just look blue to me. But now that you *have* recognised me, I must ask. Is your father around?' he whispered. 'Should I put the sunglasses back on, pronto?'

Angelina opened her mouth to tell him that her father was dead. But something stopped her. Some sudden new fear…

This man before her, this grown-up and obviously wealthy Jake might present more of a danger than the loser she'd been picturing barely an hour earlier. This man had the means to take her son away from her, in more ways than one.

She had to be very, very careful.

'You're quite safe in here,' she said, deciding she would tell him absolutely nothing of a personal nature till she'd found out more about him.

But she was extremely curious. What woman— what *mother*—wouldn't be?

The questions tumbling round in her head were almost endless, the main one being how on earth had he come to look as if he'd win the bachelor-of-the-year award in every women's magazine in Australia? And who was this Mrs Landsdale? What did she mean to Jake and how come she knew about *her*?

Despite—or perhaps because of—all these mysteries, Angelina resolved to keep her wits about her. And to act as naturally as possible.

Picking up a couple of menus, she said 'this way' with a bright smile, and showed them to what she'd always thought was the best table outside. It was to the right of the ornamental pond, with a nearby clump of tall gum trees providing natural shade. All the outdoor tables had large umbrellas, where required. But this table never needed one.

'Oh, yes, this is lovely,' Mrs Landsdale said as she sat down and glanced around. 'What a beautiful pond. And a lovely view of the valley beyond too.'

'Papa chose this spot for the restaurant because of the view. And the trees.' Too late, she wished she hadn't brought up her father.

Swiftly she handed them both menus, doing her best not to stare at Jake again. But it was hard not to. Her gaze skimmed over him once more, noting his beautifully tanned skin and the expensive gold watch on his wrist. He had money written all over him. Lots of money.

'The main-meal menu is on the front,' she explained. 'The wine list and desserts are on the back. We don't have a vast selection at any one time, but the chef does change the menu every two weeks. I can recommend the Atlantic salmon, and the rack of lamb. For dessert, the coconut pudding is to die for. I think you—'

'If you're not too busy, Angelina,' Jake interrupted, 'could you find the time to sit down and talk at some stage?'

She wanted to. Quite desperately. But pride—and common sense—refused to let her appear too eager.

'Well, we are pretty busy here on Saturdays.'

'We can't linger too long over lunch either, Jake.'
Mrs Landsdale joined in. 'The property is only open
for inspection between two and three. Maybe we
could come back here afterwards for afternoon tea
and you could catch up on old times with Angelina
then. Do you serve afternoon tea here, dear?'

Angelina didn't answer straight away, her mind
ticking over with what the woman had just said about
a property inspection. Was Jake a real-estate agent
of some kind? Or an investment adviser? What kind
of property was the woman talking about?

There were quite a few wineries for sale in the
valley at the moment, from the boutique variety to
the very large. Arnold's old place was on the market
just up the road. But he was having dreadful trouble
selling it. He'd really let the house and garden go
since his sister passed away.

There was only one way for Angelina to have all
her questions answered. And that was to ask them.
Given she'd been going to try to contact Jake anyway
in the near future, it seemed silly to pass up this
opportunity.

Yet some inner instinct was warning her to do just
that, to not let this man back into her life. Not till
Alex gave her no choice.

She searched Jake's face for a hint of the man he'd
become, then wished she hadn't. The sexual power
of his eyes was as strong as ever.

There was no use pretending she could just coldly
send him away. She had to at least talk to him.

Fortunately, she wouldn't be alone with him. This Mrs Landsdale would be there as a buffer. And a safeguard.

'We don't actually serve afternoon tea,' she said. 'But the restaurant doesn't close for lunch till four. You are quite welcome to come back after you've inspected this property, if you like. We could have a chat over coffee.'

'I'd like that,' Jake returned. 'Give me an opportunity to find out what you've been up to all these years.'

'Same here,' she replied, pleased that she could sound unconcerned, when inside she was severely agitated. 'Now, since time is of the essence, perhaps you might like to have a quick look at the menu and give me your full order straight away. Either that, or I could take your drinks order now, then send a girl over in a couple of minutes for your meal order.'

'No, no, we'll order everything right now,' the grey-haired lady said and fell to examining the menu. 'Jake, you decide on the drinks whilst I make up my mind on the food. You know my taste in wine.'

'I see you have a suggested glass of a different Ambrosia wine with each course,' Jake said as he examined the menu. 'You know, Angelina...' he rested the menu on the edge of the table and glanced up at her '...I've never seen any Ambrosia wines in bottle shops, or on Sydney restaurant wine lists. Why is that?'

'Oh. We—er—export most of our wine. Here in Australia, we've only been selling bottles at the cel-

lar door. Up till now, that is. Ambrosia Wines does
have a booth at next weekend's food and wine expo
at Darling Harbour, so hopefully we will be in some
Sydney restaurants soon.'

'I see.' Jake dropped his eyes and picked up the
menu again. 'These suggested glasses should suit
you, Dorothy. You like to try different wines. But I
won't indulge myself. Not when I'm driving. So just
mineral water for me, thanks, Angelina.'

'Flat or sparkling?' Angelina asked crisply, having
extracted her order book and Biro from her skirt
pocket.

'Sparkling, I think,' he replied. 'To match my
mood.' And he threw her a dazzling smile that sixteen years ago would have rattled her brains and sent
her heartbeat into overdrive.

Angelina's heart was still going pretty fast behind
her ribs, but her brain hadn't gone to total mush. She
flashed him back what she considered was a brilliantly cool smile, the sort of smile she could never
have produced at fifteen.

'Sparkling mineral water,' Angelina murmured as
she jotted it down. 'Now, what about your meal order?'

When she glanced up from her notebook again,
she found Jake staring at her left hand—her *ringless*
left hand. Her fingers tightened around the notebook.

'You're not married,' he said, his tone startled.

'No,' she returned in what she hoped was a crisp,
it's-really-none-of-your-business tone. 'I'm not.'

'I can't believe it! I thought you'd have half a
dozen kids by now.'

'And I thought you'd be in jail,' she countered.

Mrs Landsdale laughed. 'That's telling you, Jake. Now, stop badgering the girl and just tell her what you want to eat for now. Keep the third degree till later. But I must warn you, dear, he's the very devil when he starts questioning people. Not only is he not in jail these days, but he's also a lawyer. And a very good one, too.'

Angelina wished her mouth hadn't dropped open at this news. But Jake Winters...a *lawyer*?

'Yes, I know,' he remarked drily. 'I don't blame you for being surprised. Sometimes I'm a bit surprised myself. But Dorothy's right. We'll keep all this till later.'

Angelina digested this astonishing revelation with mixed emotions. Was this good news or bad news? She supposed it was a lot better than the father of her son being in jail. But a lawyer? She couldn't think. Too many shocks in too short a time. Best she just get on with what she was doing and think about it later.

'Have you made up your mind yet, Mrs Landsdale?' she asked the grey-haired lady.

'Do call me Dorothy,' the woman returned with a warm smile. 'And yes, I'll have the Atlantic salmon. No entrée. I'll save some room for that coconut pudding you mentioned. I'm very partial to coconut.'

'Me, too,' Angelina concurred. 'And you, Jake? Made up your mind yet?'

'The same. I'm easy.'

Angelina wanted to laugh. Easy? If there was one thing Jake Winters would never be, it was easy.

CHAPTER FOUR

SHORTLY after three, Jake jumped into his pride and joy and headed back towards the Ambrosia Estate.

Under normal circumstances, he would never leave Dorothy alone in the clutches of an eager real-estate agent on the verge of making a sale. But he could see within five minutes of Dorothy walking into that darned house that she was determined to have it. On top of that, his objections to her buying a property up here in the Hunter Valley had begun to wane.

The main reason for his change of heart lived less than a mile down this road.

Angelina Mastroianni. Unmarried, and more beautiful than ever.

Like a good wine, Angelina had only improved with age. Hard to believe she was thirty-two. She looked about twenty-five. If that.

Jake smiled when he thought of the way her big brown eyes had widened at the sight of him. Shock had mingled in their velvety depths with something else, that certain something which could not be mistaken.

She was still attracted to him, as he was still attracted to her. The sparks of sexual chemistry had flown between them all during lunch.

Frankly, Jake hadn't wanted to leave. He'd enjoyed just looking at her as she served other people, her lush Italian figure straining seductively against the crisp white blouse and hip-hugging black skirt she was wearing, especially when she bent over a bit, which was often.

As he'd sipped his mineral water, he'd imagined removing that black clip from the back of her head and watching her glossy black waves tumble in glorious disarray around her slender shoulders. Between mouthfuls of Atlantic salmon, he'd thought about slipping open the pearly buttons of her blouse and peeling it back to reveal her full breasts, those breasts which had once filled his hands. More than once he'd stared at her plum-coloured mouth and wondered if she would still be as susceptible to his kisses as she'd once been.

He'd eaten all the food she'd brought him but couldn't remember much of what it tasted like. His mind—and his appetite—had been elsewhere. Dorothy had raved about her meal and the wine afterwards, giving them both five stars. She'd raved about Angelina too, saying what a lovely girl she was and hadn't he let a good one get away all those years ago!

Jake had to agree. Angelina left all the girls he'd dated over the past few years for dead. Where they'd all been entrants in the plastic-beauty parade, Angelina Mastroianni was the real thing. Everything about her was real, from her hair to her breasts to the artless way she'd tried to hide her responses to him.

She'd failed brilliantly, making her even more attractive to him.

He was already planning to ask her out. And he wasn't going to take no for answer.

The only fly in the ointment was her father.

Jake scowled his displeasure at the thought of having to tangle with that old Italian dinosaur once more. But surely, at thirty-two, Angelina could date whomever she pleased.

If she was *free* to date, of course. Just because she wasn't married didn't mean there wasn't some man in her life.

Jake swiftly dismissed the notion of any serious competition. No woman who'd looked at him as Angelina had during lunch was madly in love with another man.

The Ferrari crested a rise and the Ambrosia Estate came into view on its left, stretching across several rolling hills, most of which were covered in vines.

There was no doubt Antonio Mastroianni had made good on his grand plans for the place. The restaurant was fabulous, positioned perfectly on the property's highest point. The guest accommodation, Jake had noted earlier from the vantage point of the restaurant car park, was further back from the main road. A modern-looking, motel-style complex, complete with swimming pool, tennis courts and lush gardens.

Sixteen years ago, that area had been nothing but bare paddocks.

The huge, barn-like structure that housed the winery itself was still on the same spot, not far from where the restaurant stood. But there were several new sheds, Jake noted as he whizzed along the road towards the main entrance. Possibly packaging and storage sheds. There was also a large dam that hadn't been there before, no doubt providing irrigation to stop the vines from becoming too stressed during droughts.

The summer he'd picked grapes here sixteen years ago had been very dry and hot, and old-man Mastroianni had talked endlessly about how stressed the vines were from lack of water. Jake had thought the notion that plants could be stressed was funny at the time. Of course, he'd been a complete idiot back then, in more ways than one.

Hopefully, Angelina would give him the opportunity to show her that he was no longer such an idiot.

His heart quickened as he turned into the restaurant car park for the second time that day. An odd happening for Jake. His heart rarely beat faster, except when he was working out or about to address a difficult jury. It rarely beat this fast over a woman.

Was he worried she might say no to him?

Yeah. He had to confess he was.

Now, that was a first.

Angelina knew the moment Jake arrived back in the car park. She'd been watching out of the corner of her eye, and that bright yellow was hard to miss. This time, thankfully, Vivien and Judith were no longer there in the restaurant to make any comments. They'd not long left after a very leisurely lunch, planning to have naps in their rooms before returning for dinner. Drinking and eating made up the mainstay of their holiday.

There were only two couples left in the restaurant, lingering over coffee. But they were seated inside. Angelina could sit outside with Jake and Dorothy, and be in no danger of being overheard, or interrupted.

She was taking a few steadying breaths and pretending to tidy up behind the counter when Jake walked in, alone. Momentarily rattled, she restrained herself from commenting till they were seated safely outside, having instructed a highly curious Wilomena to bring them both coffee and carrot cake.

'Where's Dorothy?' she asked once they were alone.

Jake took off his sunglasses and relaxed back into his chair with a sigh whilst Angelina fought the temptation to stare at him once more.

'I suspect putting a deposit down on a property up the road,' he replied drily. 'A boutique winery which has certainly seen better days. I would have stayed and tried to talk her out of it if I could. But Dorothy is one stubborn woman once she sets her sights on something. And she's set her sights on this place. The house, anyway. I left her having a second viewing and finding out the ins and outs of everything. The real-estate agent said he'd drop her off here after they were finished. He said he had to pass by on his way back to Cessnock.'

Angelina tried not to panic at this unexpected development. 'Is this house…um…white, with wide verandas?'

'That's the one.'

'Good lord, that's Arnold's place!' If Dorothy bought Arnold's place there was no hope of keeping Alex's existence a secret. The vineyard community up here was like a small town. Everyone knew everything about everyone.

Her exclamation sent Jake's dark brows arching. 'You know the owner?'

'He…um…he works for me. He's my new wine-maker.'

'I thought your father was the wine-maker here,' Jake said with a puzzled frown.

Oh, dear. Impossible now to keep secret that her father was dead. Still, everything was going to come out, sooner or later. She might as well start with the lesser revelation.

'Papa died last year,' Angelina said, and tensed in anticipation of Jake's reaction.

He said nothing for several seconds. Perhaps he was mulling over why she hadn't told him about this earlier when she had the chance.

'I'm sorry to hear that,' he said at last. 'Truly. I know how hard it is to lose someone you care about. A very good friend of mine died last year. Dorothy's husband. You don't realise how much you miss someone till they're not there for you any longer.'

Angelina was touched—and somewhat surprised—by Jake's sentiments. But at least she'd had one of her questions answered. In part. She now knew who Dorothy was. The wife of an old friend.

'How did your father die?' Jake asked. 'Had he been ill?'

'No. He was as healthy as a horse. It was quite tragic, really. He was bitten by a snake. A King Brown.'

'Good lord. That is tragic. But isn't it also unusual these days? To die of snake-bite? Don't they have antidotes?'

She nodded whilst she struggled to get a grip on herself. She hated talking about that awful day. After all, it wasn't all that long ago. Three months and a bit.

'He might have lived if he'd been bitten on the hand,' she explained. 'Or a foot. But he must have been bending over and was bitten on the chest, not far from the heart. He…he stopped breathing before the ambulance arrived. They tried to revive him but it was too late.'

Tears flooded her eyes as all the turmoil and torment of that day rushed back. Jake's reaching over the table to cover her hand with his catapulted her back to the present, and made her hotly aware that she'd been wrong this morning. Jake, the man, still had the same effect on her as Jake, the boy. When his long fingers started moving seductively against hers, a charge of electric sensations shot up her arm.

'Don't,' she snapped, and snatched her hand away from under his, clutching it firmly in her lap with her other hand.

He searched her face with thoughtful eyes. 'What's wrong, Angelina? Are you still angry with me for what happened sixteen years ago? I wouldn't blame you if you were. I was thinking earlier today how much I wanted to say sorry to you for how things turned out that night, so if it's not too late, I'm truly sorry.'

'No need for an apology,' she bit out. 'I was as much to blame as you were.'

'Then what's the problem? Why snatch your hand away like that?'

Angelina could hardly tell him the truth. That just the touch of his hand fired up her hormones as no man had in the past sixteen years. Not even close. Even now, she was looking at his mouth and wondering what it would feel like on hers again; wondering what making love would be like with him, now that he was older and so much more experienced.

Jake would be only too happy to accommodate her, she knew. Angelina had seen the way he'd looked at her during lunch today. She'd been on the end of such looks from men a lot lately. Invariably, they were followed up by some kind of pass.

She wouldn't mind betting Jake had organised leaving Dorothy behind for a while so that he could be alone with her. The realisation that he thought he could just take up with her where he'd left off all those years ago infuriated Angelina.

'You look as if you've changed, Jake,' she said sharply. 'But you haven't changed at all. You still think you can have any female you fancy.'

He smiled the most heart-stopping smile. 'It would be hard not to fancy you, Angelina. You were a gorgeous-looking girl, but you're one stunning-looking woman.'

Angelina gritted her teeth to stop herself from smiling back at him. Damn the man, he was incorrigible. And almost irresistible.

Wilomena arriving with the coffee and cake was a godsend. But she was gone all too soon.

'This is great cake,' Jake praised after his first mouthful.

'Glad you like it,' she remarked snippily.

He took another mouthful, followed up by some coffee. She watched him, her own appetite nil, her frustration growing. Who did he think he was? It would serve him right if she upped and told him right now the result of his last encounter with her. Finding out he had a fifteen-year-old son was sure to wipe that satisfied look off his far too handsome face.

But she didn't tell him. She couldn't be sure of his reaction, and there was no way she was going to upset Alex this year. Angelina aimed to delay Jake finding out about his son as long as possible.

'So!' Jake exclaimed, dabbing at his mouth with a serviette after polishing off his slice of cake and most of his coffee. 'Is there a current man in your life, Angelina? Or are you footloose and fancy-free?'

Here comes the pass, she thought irritably. Well, he was in for a surprise because she intended to head him off at the pass. As much as Jake still had the power to turn her head—and turn her on—Angelina wasn't about to fall for his smooth but empty line of patter twice in one lifetime.

'Yes, of course there's a man in my life,' came her blithe reply. Alex was almost a man after all.

Jake muttered something under his breath before searching her face again with those hard, sexy blue eyes of his. 'So what's the score? Is it serious? Are you living with him?'

'Sometimes.'

'Sometimes.' Jake looked puzzled. 'What does that mean?'

'He lives in Sydney most of the time. Comes up here for holidays and the occasional weekend. And I go down there to see him every once in a while.'

'What about next weekend? Will you be seeing him next weekend?'

'Nope. I'll be attending the food and wine expo at Darling Harbour.'

'You mean you'll be in Sydney and you're not going to see each other, not even at *night*?'

Angelina couldn't decide if she found Jake's shock amusing or annoying. Clearly, his priority in a relationship was still sex.

'Alex will be away next weekend,' she said coolly. Actually, Alex was going to a special swimming training camp in preparation for the big interschool swimming carnival the following weekend. He was the captain of the team. 'I'll be seeing him the following weekend.' At the swimming carnival.

'Where are you staying this weekend in Sydney?'

Angelina almost laughed. Obviously, Jake didn't aim to go quietly off into the sunset. She should have known.

'I've booked a room at the Star City Casino for Saturday night,' came her composed reply. 'It's the closest hotel to the expo.' In truth, she wasn't strictly needed at the expo. The marketing agency who now handled the Ambrosia Estate account had hired professional sales people for the weekend. But she thought it wise to check personally on how her money was being spent. This venture hadn't been cheap.

But Angelina knew you had to invest money to make money these days. It had been her idea for the winery to get a web site two years ago. Her father had argued against the idea, but she'd had her way and it had brought them in a lot of business.

'Are you planning to marry this Alex one day?' Jake asked abruptly.

'No.'

Jake shook his head, his expression bewildered. 'That's what I don't get with you, Angelina. Why *haven't* you got married? I thought marriage and children were a must with Italian girls.'

'Not with me. I have other priorities.' *Like our son.* 'Now that Papa's gone, I'm solely responsible for the running of this place. That's a lot of work. But enough about me. What about you, Jake?' she asked, swiftly deflecting the conversation away from her own personal life and on to his. 'Are you married?'

The corner of his mouth tipped up in a wry smile. 'Come, now, Angelina. I told you way back when I was seventeen that I would never get married. I've had no reason to change my mind on that score.'

Her heart sinking at this news annoyed her. What had she subconsciously been hoping could happen here? That he would fall madly in love with her this time, marry her and they would live happily ever after, the three of them?

Dream on, Angelina.

'What about children?' she couldn't resist asking. 'Haven't you ever wanted a son? Or a daughter?' she added quickly.

'God, no. I'd be a simply dreadful father. Just the thought of being responsible for a child's upbringing gives me nightmares.'

Oh, great, she thought. He's going to be thrilled when he finds out about Alex. It was as well Alex was almost grown up, if that was Jake's attitude.

'Why do you say you'd be a dreadful father?' she asked, though she suspected it had something to do with his childhood. He'd never told her specifics all those years ago, but she'd been left with the impression of serious neglect.

Angelina's father had always been a right pain in

the neck, but he'd never left her in any doubt that he loved her.

'I'm way too selfish for starters,' he confessed. 'And damaged, Dorothy would say. You know the theory. An abused child often becomes an abusive parent. But let's not talk about life's little nasties,' he swept on, brushing aside any further explanation. 'Let's talk about you instead. OK, so you don't want the traditional role of wife and mother. I can accept that. I guess you have got your hands pretty full running this place. A lot of women these days are into the business scene. And careers. Don't go imagining I'd ever judge you harshly for that.'

'How generous of you,' came her caustic retort.

He just smiled at her again, as though amused by her impertinence.

'So when are you going to dump that loser you've been seeing and go out with me?'

Now Angelina did laugh. The man had the hide of an elephant. Exasperated, she decided to prick his ego some more. 'Alex is no loser. He's just as good-looking as you are. And just as successful, I might add. In fact, he's the only son and heir to a veritable fortune.' Besides being worth millions—property-wise—the Ambrosia Estate ran at a tidy profit each year, with their resort and restaurant very popular, and their wines in high demand over in America and Europe. If Angelina's plans for expansion into more markets bore fruit, profits could be even higher in future.

'Not impressed,' Jake countered confidently. 'Money

is nothing. Attitude is everything. He's a loser. Because if you were my woman,' Jake said, and leant closer to her across the table, 'I'd make damned sure I wasn't away if you were going to be in Sydney next weekend. You wouldn't be staying at some hotel on Saturday night, either. You'd be staying at my place.'

His eyes locked on to hers and for the life of her, she could not look away. In the end, she laughed again. It was the only way she could safely draw air into her suddenly starving lungs.

'But I'm not your woman, am I?'

He leant back in his seat again, still holding her eyes firmly captive with his. 'What if I said I wanted you to be, more than anything I've wanted in a long time? What if I told you to tell this Alex he's history? What if I asked you to stay at my place next weekend instead of the Casino?'

She should have protested at that point. But she was too enthralled with thinking about what it would be like to spend next weekend with him, staying at his place.

'I have this wonderful harbourside apartment with all the mod cons and only a short ferry ride to Darling Harbour,' he went on when she foolishly stayed silent. 'We could paint the town red on Saturday night, or stay in, if you prefer. Then on Sunday we could have lunch down on the waterfront somewhere. You must surely get a lunch break. Unfortunately, I have to be in court first thing

Monday morning, or we could have made it a long weekend.'

Angelina finally found her voice. 'What is it you expect me to say to these extraordinarily presumptuous suggestions?'

'Right now? Nothing. I wouldn't like to be accused of rushing you into anything, like last time. I'll call you later this week. Or you can call me earlier than that, if you'd like. Here...' He whipped out his wallet from his jeans and extracted two business cards. 'You got a pen on you?'

She did, in fact. She kept one in her skirt pocket. She fished it out and gave it to him. He flashed her a quick smile before bending to the task of adding some numbers to the first card before handing it over. 'That first number is my private and unlisted number at home. The second is my cellphone. Now, write yours down for me on this...' And he handed her a second card, along with the Biro.

She stared down at the white card which said simply 'Jake Winters, Lawyer' in bold black letters, along with an office address and phone number in smaller lettering underneath.

She turned it over and jotted down both her numbers, all the while thinking to herself, what *was* she doing?

She wasn't going to say yes to his invitation. How could she? OK, so she was tempted. She was only human. What woman wouldn't respond to what Jake was making her feel at this moment? As if she was the most beautiful, most desirable girl he'd ever met.

What had he said? That he wanted her to be his woman more than anything he'd wanted in a long time.

The devil would be proud of him!

Sixteen years ago, she'd fallen for such a line, hook, line and sinker. Well, she *had*, hadn't she? But sixteen years had taught Angelina to recognise the signs of a dedicated womaniser. You didn't have to have jumped into bed with that type to recognise their trappings. Jake had them all. The car. The clothes. And the charm.

Angelina knew beyond a doubt that being Jake's woman was only a temporary position, whereas her being Alex's mother was forever. Allowing herself to be seduced a second time by Alex's father was just not on.

At the same time, she *was* curious to learn a little more about him, and his life. This was the man she was going to have to entrust her son to, possibly sooner than she'd anticipated. After all, once Dorothy moved up here and found out dear Angelina at the Ambrosia Estate was a single mum with a fifteen-year-old son who just happened to be the dead spit of Jake, the cat would be out of the bag. And as much as Jake might try to abdicate his responsibilities where Alex was concerned, Angelina knew that her stubborn son would not let him get away with that. No, Alex would force himself into Jake's life whether Jake wanted it or not.

'I'm not promising anything,' she remarked coolly as she handed back the card. 'But you're welcome to ring me. I might agree to have lunch with you. Alex wouldn't mind my having lunch with an old friend.'

'I'm sure he won't,' Jake said as he tucked the card back into his wallet. 'It's hardly a grand passion between you two, is it?'

'You know nothing about my relationship with Alex.'

'I know enough,' he stated with an arrogance which was as unsettling as it was wickedly attractive. Why, oh, why did she have to find him so exciting?

Maybe she shouldn't agree to lunch with him. Even lunch might be a worry, especially down at Darling Harbour, with its air of away-from-home glamour and glitz. Sydney could be a very seductive city. Angelina often found herself losing her head a bit when she was there and spending more money than she should. Especially on clothes. She had a wardrobe full of lovely things she rarely wore.

She would have to weigh up the pros and cons of lunching with Jake before his call. If she thought there was any danger of making a fool of herself, she would not go.

'I'll look forward to ringing you,' Jake said, and slipped his wallet into the back pocket of his jeans. 'Meanwhile, surely you have some questions for yours truly? Don't you want to know how come I'm a lawyer and not in jail?'

Angelina shook her head at him in frustration. He was like a rolling bulldozer, difficult to stop.

'I'm sure you're going to tell me, whether I want to hear or not.'

'You *want* to hear,' he said cheekily. 'You know you do.'

So Angelina listened—yes, in rapt silence—whilst he told her everything that had happened to him since that fateful night. She marvelled at his good fortune, and couldn't help feeling a bit proud of him. Both Dorothy and her husband had clearly been wonderful, but Jake must have worked very hard to accomplish what he had.

Not that she intended telling him that. He was smug enough as it was.

'And to think I worried myself sick that I'd been responsible for your going to jail,' she said when he finished his tale of miracles.

'Did you really? Oh, that's sweet. But you were sweet back then. Very sweet.'

'Don't count on my being so sweet now, lover-boy. I've grown up. I might not live in the big bad city but a number of Sydney's more successful swinging singles have stayed at the Ambrosia Estate over the years. I know all about men like you.'

He laughed. 'Tell me about men like me.'

'You work hard and you play hard.'

'True.' He picked up his coffee-cup again.

'You like your own way and you don't always stick to the rules.'

'Mmm. True, I guess.' And smiled at her over the rim of the cup.

'You're all commitment-phobic sex addicts who change girlfriends as often as you do your cars.'

Jake almost choked on the last of his coffee. 'Now, wait here,' he spluttered. 'That's not quite true.'

'Which part is not quite true?' she asked tartly.

'I've only had two cars in the last few years. A navy Mazda and the yellow Ferrari I'm driving today.'

'Surprising. OK, so what's the girlfriend count during that time?'

He looked a bit sheepish. 'I don't have that many fingers and toes. But what about you, Miss Tough Cookie? Or shouldn't I ask?'

No way could she let him find out there hadn't been anyone since him. His ego would probably explode. And his predatory nature would go into full pursuit mode.

'You can ask, but I'm not into the kiss-and-tell scene,' she tossed off. 'Let's just say I'm a big girl now and I run my own race.'

'Even when your father was alive?'

'After my not-so-successful rendezvous with you, I learned to be more sneaky.'

'You'd have to be with a father like yours around,' came his rueful remark. 'So! Did your dad *like* this Alex of yours? Or didn't he know about him?'

'He adored Alex.' Too late, Angelina wished she hadn't started that silly subterfuge.

'An Italian, is he?' Jake said drily.

'Half. Now, no more questions about Alex, please. Aah, Dorothy's back,' she said, spying the lady herself walking along the path towards them, accompanied by a portly, grey-haired man in his fifties. 'She seems to have brought the real-estate agent with her.' Fortunately, not one Angelina knew personally.

But when Dorothy swept in with the news she had secured the property and that she was here to get the owner's signature on some papers, a panic-stricken Angelina jumped to her feet and offered to find Arnold for them.

'But why don't you want them to know about Alex?' Arnold said when she cornered him in the barrel room of the winery five minutes later.

'The man with the woman who's buying your place is Alex's father,' Angelina explained reluctantly. 'All right?'

Arnold's eyes rounded. 'Heaven be praised! Just as well Antonio isn't here, or there'd be hell to pay. But he's not here, Angelina, so why keep the boy a secret?'

'Only for a little while, Arnold. I will tell Jake. But in my own good time. OK?'

'Has this Jake turned into a decent kind of chap?'

Decent. Now, decent was a subjective word.

'He's a lawyer,' she said.

'Nothing wrong with lawyers. At least he's got a job. Things could be worse.'

Angelina nodded. 'You're so right. Things *could* be worse.'

But not much.

CHAPTER FIVE

'YOU don't look too pleased,' Dorothy said within seconds of leaving the Ambrosia Estate. 'Did the lovely Angelina surprise you this time by saying no?'

Jake's hands tightened on the steering wheel. 'Things didn't go exactly according to plan. But I haven't given up yet.'

'Good.'

Jake's eyes slanted over towards Dorothy. 'You mean my old flame has your tick of approval?'

'She's a big improvement on your last few girl-friends,' Dorothy said in her usual droll fashion. 'And she'd be very convenient, considering where I'll be living soon. I'll have no worries about seeing you regularly if you start going out with a local girl.'

'I have to get her to drop some guy named Alex first.'

'You've never had any trouble getting your girl-friends to drop their old boyfriends before.'

'This one sounds formidable. A poor little rich boy. Very good-looking. Lives in Sydney. Too bad I didn't find out his last name. I could have had him investigated. From the sound of things, they don't get together all that often. He's probably two-timing her with some city chick. Guys like that are never faithful.'

'You'd know.'

'Dorothy Landsdale, I'll have you know I've always been faithful to my girlfriends!'

'Oh, I don't doubt it. They don't last long enough for you to do the dirty on them. Every few weeks it's out with the old and in with the new.'

Jake didn't like the flavour of this conversation. Dorothy was making him sound as if he was some kind of serial sleazebag where women were concerned. Angelina had inferred the same thing.

'I can well understand Angelina not jumping at the chance of being next in line,' Dorothy went on before Jake could defend himself. 'She might like a bit more security in her relationships. And a possible future.'

'I'll have you know she's no more interested in marriage and having a family than I am. She told me so. She's a career girl.'

'What? Oh, I find that hard to believe. That girl has marriage and motherhood written all over her.'

'You're just saying that because she's Italian.'

'Not at all. I've known enough career women in my life to recognise one when I meet her. If Angelina Mastroianni is a career woman, then I'm...I'm Marilyn Monroe!'

Jake laughed. 'In that case, perhaps I should be relieved that she said no to me.'

'Perhaps you should.'

But he wasn't relieved. He was annoyed. And frustrated. And jealous as hell of this Alex bloke.

Angelina belonged to *him*. She'd always belonged to him.

The sudden primitiveness—and *possessiveness*—of his thoughts stunned Jake. This wasn't him. This was some other man, some caveman who believed that his taking a female's virginity gave him the rights to her body forever.

Logic told Jake this was crazy thinking. But logic wasn't worth a damn beside the passion and determination that was firing Jake's belly at this moment. She was going to be his again. That Alex guy was going to be history, no matter what it took!

Angelina watched the yellow car till it disappeared from view, then she turned and walked with slow steps back down the path to the restaurant.

Wilomena—who had no doubt been waiting with bated breath to collar her alone—pounced immediately. A tall, rake-thin brunette, the restaurant's head waitress had sharp eyes to go with her sharp features.

'All right, fess up, Angelina? Who was that gorgeous hunk in the yellow Ferrari?'

'Just a guy I used to know. No one special.'

'Just a guy you used to know,' Wilomena repeated with rolling eyes. 'Did you hear that, Kevin?' she called out to the chef, who was the only other staff member left in the restaurant at this hour. The rest of the evening's waitresses wouldn't arrive till five-thirty, which was almost an hour away. 'He was just a guy she used to know. No one special.'

Kevin popped his bald head round the doorway that connected the body of the restaurant with the kitchen. In his late thirties, Kevin was English and single and a simply brilliant chef. He'd been on a working holiday around Australia a few years ago, filled in for their chef, who'd been taken ill, and never left. Since his arrival the restaurant's reputation had gone from good to great.

'Amazing how much he looked like Alex, isn't it?' Kevin said with a straight face. 'If I didn't know better, I would have said he was Alex's father.'

Angelina groaned. It was no use. She had no hope of keeping Jake's identity a secret, not even for a minute.

'It's all right,' Wilomena said gently when she saw the distress on her boss's face. 'We won't say anything. Not if you don't want us to.'

'I don't want you to,' Angelina returned pleadingly. 'Not yet, anyway. The other girls didn't notice, did they?'

'No. They're too new. And too silly. All they can think about on a Saturday is where they're going tonight, and with whom. So! Does he know about Alex? Is that why he was here?'

'No. He has no idea. He just dropped in for lunch by sheer accident and he…he…. Oh, Wilomena, it's terribly complicated.'

'Why don't you sit down and tell me all about it?'

Angelina looked at Wilomena, who at thirty-eight had a few years on her. Divorced, with two teenage girls, she lived in Cessnock and worked long hours at the restaurant six days a week to support herself and her kids. Angelina realised she could do worse than confide in Wilomena, who was both pragmatic and practical. And she needed someone to confide in. The only friends she had now were the people she worked with. Her father had been her best friend. Still, this little problem wasn't something she'd have been able to talk to him about. He'd been totally blind when it came to the subject of Jake Winters.

'OK,' she said with a sigh. 'Let's have a glass of wine and I'll tell you all.'

Wilomena smiled. She was really quite attractive when she smiled. 'Fantastic. Let's go into the kitchen so Kevin can hear. Otherwise, I'll just have to repeat everything after you've gone.'

Angelina laughed. 'You two are getting as thick as thieves, aren't you?'

'Yeah,' Wilomena said with a twinkle in her quick blue eyes. 'We are.'

Half an hour later, Angelina made her way slowly along the path that ran from the restaurant and past the cellar door before branching into two paths. One led to the winery, the other followed the driveway that led to the resort proper, a distance of about a hundred metres. She headed for the resort, her shoes crunching on the gravel, her head down in thought as she walked down the gentle incline.

Kevin had advised her to tell Jake the truth as soon as possible, especially since Alex himself wanted to meet his father. He'd said he would want to know if he had a son and would be seriously annoyed if such news was held back from him.

'And that's bulldust about this Jake saying he'd be

a rotten father,' Kevin had pronounced. 'Lots of men talk like that. You wait till he finds out he has a son for real, especially a great kid like Alex. He'll be falling over himself to be the best father he possibly can.'

Wilomena hadn't shared Kevin's optimism. There again, she had more jaundiced views about the opposite sex and their ability to be good fathers.

'What fantasyland do you live in, Kevin?' she'd countered tartly. 'Obviously, you've never been a father. From my experience, lots of men these days soon get very bored with the day-to-day responsibilities of fatherhood. Guys like Jake, especially. He admitted to Angelina he was selfish. And damaged, whatever that means. I think Angelina's right to be careful. I don't think she should tell him anything for a while. If nothing else, it gives Alex time to grow up some more. It'll be weeks before this Dorothy lady moves up here. Meanwhile, Arnold's not going to say anything.'

They'd argued back and forth, with Angelina a bemused onlooker. In the end, Kevin had thrown up his hands and told Wilomena it was no wonder she was still single, if she was so distrusting and contemptuous of men.

Angelina had done her best to smooth things over between them but by the time she'd left, there'd been a chilling silence in the kitchen. She was relieved she wasn't working there tonight. Or on the reception desk. She'd already planned to take the evening off, to do some female things, like have a long bath, shave her legs, put a treatment in her hair and do her nails. It would be good to be alone, to think.

'Angelina, Angelina!'

Angelina turned to find Wilomena running after her.

'Sorry about the ruckus in there,' Wilomena said on reaching her. 'Don't worry about it. Kevin will be fine later tonight. And yes, before you ask, we are sleeping together.'

'I...I wasn't going to ask.'

Wilomena frowned. 'No, you wouldn't, would you? You're not like other girls. It almost killed you to tell us what you told us in there, didn't it? I mean, you're not one to gossip, or to confide.'

'No, I...I guess not.' When you spent the amount of time *she* had spent alone, you lost the knack of confiding in other people. You tried to solve your problems yourself.

'Look, I just wanted to say that I think you should go out with Jake, but without telling him about Alex. Aside from having a bit of long-overdue fun, you can go see where Jake lives, and how he lives. See what kind of man he is.'

'But how did you...?'

'Yeah, I know, you didn't tell us he'd asked you out. But I didn't come down in the last shower, honey, and I watched you two today. Both times. He asked you out all right and you said no, didn't you?'

'I haven't actually given him an answer yet.'

'What does he want you to do?'

'Stay at his place when I go to Sydney for the expo next weekend.'

'Wow. He's a fast mover all right. It took Kevin two years to ask me out, then two months to get me in the sack.'

'It took Jake about two minutes the first time,' Angelina said drily.

'Ooooh. That good, eh?'

'His kisses were. The sex itself was not great. I froze, and he just went ahead.'

'But you wouldn't freeze this time,' Wilomena said intuitively.

Angelina stiffened. 'I have no intention of finding out if I would or I wouldn't. And I have no intention of staying at his place next weekend.'

'But why not? I wouldn't be able to resist, if it were me. The guy's a hunk of the first order.'

Angelina didn't need to be told that. Jake, the man, had even more sex appeal than Jake, the bad boy. And *he'd* had oodles.

'If it was anyone other than Alex's father, I would.'

'If it was anyone other than Alex's father, you wouldn't want to,' Wilomena said. 'I've known girls like you before, Angelina. You're a one-man woman. And he's the man.'

'That's romantic nonsense!'

'Is it?' Wilomena probed softly.

'Yes,' Angelina said stubbornly whilst secretly thinking that Wilomena could be right. Why else hadn't she accepted dates with other men? It wasn't as though she hadn't been asked. She couldn't even claim to be protecting Alex any more, now that he was at boarding school most of the time.

Wilomena shrugged. 'Have it your way. So, you're really not going to see Jake next weekend? Not at all?'

'I…I might go to lunch with him.'

The look on Wilomena's face was telling.

'Just lunch!' Angelina insisted. 'As you yourself said, I need to find out some more about him.'

'Sounds like an excuse to gaze at him some more.'

'I didn't gaze at him today. I was just shocked at how much he looks like Alex.'

'Who do you think you're kidding?'

Angelina groaned. 'I did stare, didn't I?'

'Don't beat yourself up over it. The man was worth a stare. I ogled myself. So did every other woman in the place.'

'Which is why I can't risk being alone with him again. The man's a right devil where women are concerned. He always was.'

'Mmm. But aren't you curious over what it would be like with him now? I mean, he's sure to be very good in the sack. If what you say about him is true, he's had plenty of practice.'

'Too much practice. No, I'm not curious about his lovemaking abilities,' she lied. 'Only about his character and whether he's going to be good for Alex.'

'You know, Angelina, you're a woman as well as a mother. Do you ever think of your own needs?'

'Yes, of course I do.'

'But I've never known you to go out on a date. Not during the time I've worked here, anyway.'

'Dating is seriously overrated. And so is sex.'

'Don't knock it till you try it.'

Angelina flushed. 'Who says I haven't?'

'I have eyes, honey. And ears. If you'd slept with someone around here, I'd know about it. Look, your father's gone now and Alex is almost grown up. Time for you to live a little.'

'Maybe. But not with Jake.' *I'd probably fall in love with him again and then where would I be?*

'Yeah, perhaps you're right. If you slept with him, it could be awkward once he finds out about Alex. He might think you were trying to trap him into marriage.'

'I'd be more concerned over what Alex thought.'

'I dare say you would. You're a very good mother, Angelina. You put me to shame sometimes.'

'Nonsense. You're a great mother.'

'I try to be. Talking of kids, I have to go and ring mine. See what the little devils are up to.'

'And I have to ring Alex and see how he did at cricket today.'

'Being a mother just never stops, does it?' And with a parting grin, Wilomena hurried off.

Angelina sighed and made her way down the rest of the path and through the covered archway that provided protection for arriving guests. A green Jaguar was parked there, with a middle-aged couple inside booking in. Angelina slipped through a side-gate just past Reception that led into a private courtyard attached to the manager's quarters, a spacious two-bedroomed unit with an *en suite* to the main.

She and Alex had moved in there two years ago after Angelina had started doing night shifts at the reception desk. The excuse she'd used for the move was that the old farmhouse where they'd been living, and where she'd been born and brought up, was a couple of hundred metres away, far too long a walk for her at night. Or so she had told her father. Papa had not been happy with their move at first, but he'd got used to it. Besides, when Alex came home on holiday, he'd often stayed with his grandfather in his old room.

Angelina rarely ventured back there, the house not having all that many good memories for her. She'd been a lonely child living there, and an even lonelier single mother. She much preferred her memoryless apartment with its fresh cream walls, cream floor coverings and all mod cons. She liked the modern furniture too, having never been fond of the heavy and ornate furniture her father had preferred. Now that her father was gone, Arnold was living in the old farmhouse, free accommodation being part of his contract as Ambrosia's wine-maker.

Of course, Alex hadn't liked that at all, having someone else living in his grandfather's house. But that was just too bad.

Another sigh escaped Angelina's lips as she let herself in the front door. What a day it had been so far. And it wasn't over yet.

She moved straight across the cream carpet to the

side-table where she kept the phone, sitting down on the green and cream checked sofa and calling Alex on his cellphone. He should have finished playing cricket by now.

'Yes, Mum,' he answered after the second ring.

'You lost,' she said, knowing that tone of voice.

'I don't want to talk about it,' he grumped.

'Never mind. You'll wallop them at the swimming carnival.'

'We'd better. They'll be insufferable if they win that, too.'

Alex had a killer competitive instinct. He was the one who would be insufferable.

'So how's things up there?' he asked.

'Everything's fine. Arnold sold his place today.' *And your father showed up out of the blue.*

Alex groaned. 'Does that mean we're stuck with him forever?'

'Alex, I'm not sure what your problem is with Arnold. He's a really nice man. You could learn a lot from him. Your grandfather said he was brilliant with whites. You know Papa was not at his best with whites. He was more of a red man. But no, we're not stuck with him forever. He said he's going to buy a little place over in Port Stephens with what he gets for his place, with enough left over for his retirement. He's well aware how keen you are to take over and is more than willing to stand aside when you feel ready to take on the job of wine-maker.'

'Good. Because I intend to do just that as soon as I finish my higher-school certificate.'

A prickle ran down Angelina's spine. He sounded like Jake had today. So strong and so determined.

'I won't stand in your way, Alex,' she said. 'This place is your inheritance, and the job of wine-maker is your right.'

'And I'm going to find my father, too. Not in November. I can't wait that long. I'm going to start next holidays. At Easter.'

Angelina grimaced. Easter! That was only a few weeks away. Still, maybe it was for the best. She couldn't stand the tension of such a long wait herself.

'All right, Alex. You'll get no further argument from me on that score. Come Easter, we'll go find your father.'

'Honest?' Alex sounded amazed. 'You're not going to make a fuss?'

'No.'

'Cool. You're the best, Mum.'

'Mmm.'

'Got to go. The dinner bell's gone. Love ya.'

'Love you, too,' she replied, but he'd already hung up.

Tears filled her eyes as she hung up too.

'Lord knows what you're crying over, Angelina,' she muttered. 'Things could be worse, as Arnold said.'

But she wasn't entirely convinced.

CHAPTER SIX

JAKE paced back and forth across his living room, unable to eat, unable to sit and watch television or work or do any of the other activities that usually filled his alone-time.

The sleek, round, silver-framed clock on the wall pronounced that it was getting on for half-past eight. He'd dropped Dorothy off at her place in Rose Bay at seven-thirty, an hour earlier. The drive back from the Hunter Valley had taken a lot longer than the drive up. They'd been caught up in the Saturday-night traffic coming into the city, slowing to a crawl near the Harbour Bridge.

'I won't miss this when I move to the country,' Dorothy had declared impatiently, which had rather amused Jake at the time. She should see how bad the traffic was in peak hours on a weekday. If there was an accident on the bridge, or in the tunnel, the lines of traffic didn't crawl. They just stopped.

But that was city living for you.

Jake had declined Dorothy's invitation to come in for a bite to eat, and now here he was, unfed and unable to relax, becoming increasingly agitated and angry. With himself.

He'd handled Angelina all wrong today. He'd come on to her way too strong, and way too fast.

That might work with city babes in wine bars on a Friday night, but not girls like Angelina. Even when she was fifteen, she hadn't been easy. She'd made him wait, forcing him to make endless small talk that summer before finally agreeing to meet him alone.

He could see now that her still being attracted to him in a physical sense wasn't enough for her to drop her current boyfriend and go out with him. She claimed she was a modern woman who'd been around, but he suspected—like Dorothy—that Angelina was not as sophisticated as she thought she was. She had an old-fashioned core.

She was going to say no when he finally rang her. Nothing was surer in his mind. And the prospect was killing him.

He had to change his tactics. Hell, he was a smart guy, wasn't he? A lawyer. Changing tactics midstream came naturally to him.

Go back to square one, Jake. Chat her up some more. Show her your warm and sensitive side. You have to have one. Edward said you did. Then you might stand a chance of winning, if not her heart, then her body.

And don't wait till tomorrow night to call. Do it now. Right now, buddy, whilst she can still remember how it felt today when you touched her hand, and looked deep into her eyes and talked about spending a whole weekend together.

If it was even remotely what you felt—what you are *still* feeling—then she has to be tempted.

Jake's hand was unsteady as he took out his wallet

and extracted the card where she'd written down her telephone numbers. He had it bad all right. It had been a long time since he'd felt this desperate over a woman. Damn it all, he'd *never* felt this desperate before!

Except perhaps that summer sixteen years ago. He'd been desperate for Angelina back then too. No wonder he'd been hopeless by the time he'd actually done it with her.

Jake craved the opportunity to show her he wasn't a hopeless lover now.

But first, he had to get her to say yes to seeing him again. Even lunch would do. She'd said she might go to lunch with him. It wasn't quite what he had in mind but it was a start.

He dragged in several deep breaths as he walked over to sweep up the receiver of his phone. His hand was only marginally steadier as he punched in her number but he consoled himself with the fact she could not see it shake.

As long as he sounded calm. And sincere. That was all that mattered.

Angelina was sitting on the sofa and painting her toenails, her right foot propped up on the glass coffee-table, when the phone rang. The brush immediately zigzagged across her second toe onto her big toe, leaving a long streak of plum nail-polish on her skin.

The swear-word she uttered was not one she would

have used if Alex had been home. Or if her father had been alive.

By the time she replaced the brush in the bottle, poured some remover on a cotton-wool ball and wiped off the wayward polish, then leant over to snatch up the phone from the nearby side-table, it had been ringing for quite a while.

'Yes?' she answered sharply. She hoped it wasn't Wilomena with more advice. She was all adviced out. Besides, she'd already made up her mind what she was going to say to Jake when he finally rang.

'Angelina? It's Jake. Have I rung at an awkward moment?'

Jake. It was Jake!

'You weren't supposed to ring till later in the week,' she snapped, hating it that just the sound of his voice could make her stomach go all squishy.

'I couldn't wait till then to apologise,' he said. 'I wouldn't have been able to sleep tonight.'

'Apologise for what?' Her voice was still sharp.

His, however, was soft and seductive.

'I was out of line today.'

'Were you really?' Now her tone was dry, and sarcastic.

No way was she going to be all sweetness and light. She was still seriously annoyed with him for turning up in her life at this particular point in time and making her make difficult decisions.

'I was pushy and presumptuous, as you said. My only excuse is that I didn't want to let you get away from me a second time. I really liked you sixteen years ago, Angelina, but I like the woman you've become even better.'

She laughed. 'Wow, you've really become the master of the polished line, haven't you? But you can save the flattery for another occasion, Jake. I've already decided to have lunch with you on Saturday.'

The dead silence on the other end of the line gave Angelina some satisfaction that she'd been able to knock him speechless. Unfortunately, now that she'd voiced her decision out loud to him, the reality of it shook her right down to her half-painted toes.

But the die had been rolled. No going back.

'Great!' he said, sounding much too happy for her liking. 'I'm already looking forward to it. But does— er—Alex know?'

'I spoke to him earlier this evening. We talked about you.'

'What did you say? I'll bet you didn't tell him how we first met.'

'Alex already knows all about you, Jake. There are no secrets between us.'

'And he *agreed* to your going to lunch with me?'

'Why should he object to a platonic lunch between old friends?'

'Old *flames*, Angelina. Not old friends.'

'Whatever. A lot of water has gone under the bridge since then, Jake.'

'I'll bet you didn't tell him everything I said to you today.'

What could she say to that?

'You didn't, did you?' Jake continued when she

remained silent. 'No man—not even your pathetic Alex—would willingly let his girlfriend go to lunch with another man who'd declared his wish to make her *his* woman.'

Angelina could not believe the passion in Jake's words. And the power. How easy it would be to forget all common sense and tell him that she had changed her mind, that she would not only go to lunch with him on Saturday, but she would also stay at his place on the Saturday night.

Dear heaven, she *was* going to make a fool of herself with him again. Or she might, if she went to lunch with him on Saturday as things stood. If he could do this to her over the phone, what could he do to her when she was alone with him in the big bad city?

She had to tell him about Alex. Right here and now. It was the only way she could protect herself against her susceptibility to this man.

'Jake, there's something I have to tell you,' she began, then stopped as she struggled for the right words. He was going to be shocked out of his mind. And furious with her for playing word games with him. How she could possibly explain why she'd done such a thing? She was going to look a fool, no matter what she said, or did.

'Alex doesn't know you're going to lunch with me at all, does he?' Jake jumped in.

'Er—no. He doesn't.'

'You realise what that means, Angelina. You're

finished with him, whether you admit it or not. You're not the sort of girl to two-time a guy.'

'I don't consider lunch a two-timing act,' she argued, panicking at the way this conversation was now going. Instead of finding sanctuary in the truth, she was getting in deeper. And deeper.

'It is when you know that the guy you're having lunch with wants more than to share a meal with you,' Jake pointed out ruefully.

'But what *you* want is not necessarily what *I* want,' she countered, stung by his presumption.

'That's not the impression you gave me today. We shared something special once, Angelina. It's still there. The sparks. The chemistry.'

'Men like you share a chemistry with lots of women, Jake. It's nothing special. Which reminds me, is there some current girlfriend who should know that you've asked another woman out to lunch?'

'No.'

'Why not?'

'I'm between girlfriends at the moment.'

She laughed. 'Am I supposed to believe that?'

'You sure are. I'm a lot of things but I'm no liar.'

'Such as what? What are you, Jake Winters, that I should worry about before daring to go to lunch with you?'

'You don't honestly expect me to put myself down, do you? I'm no saint but I'm not one of the bad guys, either. I don't lie and I don't cheat. There is no other woman in my life. But I *am* a confirmed bachelor. And I aim to stay that way. Which should please you, since you're not into wedding bells and baby bootees. Or did I get that wrong?'

'No. No, you didn't get that wrong.'

If I can't marry you, then I don't want to marry anyone.

The thought burst into her mind. Shocking her. *Shattering* her. This couldn't be. This wasn't fair. Not only that, but it was also crazy. He'd only been in her life a few short hours this time.

She couldn't be in love with him again. Not really. She was being confused and corrupted by the romance of the situation. And by desire. His, as well as her own. She wasn't sure which was the more powerful. Being wanted the way Jake said he wanted her. Or her wanting him.

Angelina still could not believe the feelings which had rampaged through her when he'd simply touched her hand.

Wilomena was probably right. She was a one-man woman.

And Jake was the man. Impossible to resist him. She could go to lunch with him next Saturday, pretending that it was a reconnaissance mission to find out what kind of man he was. But that was all it would be. A pretence.

'Tell me about your job,' she said, valiantly resolving to put their conversation back on to a more platonic, getting-to-know-you basis. 'What kind of lawyer are you?'

'A darned good one.'

'No, I mean what kind of people do you represent?'

'People who need a good lawyer to go in to bat for them. People who've been put down and put upon, usually in the corporate world. Employees who've been unfairly dismissed, or sexually harassed, or made to endure untenable work conditions. I have this woman client at the moment who's in the process of suing her boss. She worked as his assistant in an un-air-conditioned office with him for years whilst he chain-smoked. She repeatedly asked him to put her in a separate office but he wouldn't. Yet he was filthy rich. She now has terminal lung cancer and she's only forty-two. We're suing for millions. And we'll win, too.'

'But she won't,' Angelina said. 'She'll die.'

'Yes, she'll die. But her teenage children won't. She told me she'd die happier if she gets enough money to provide for them till they can provide for themselves. Her husband's an invalid as well. That's why she had to work and why she stayed working for that bastard under such rotten conditions. Because the job was within walking distance of her house, and she didn't have a car. She couldn't afford one.'

'That's so sad. I hate hearing stories like that. Don't tell me any more, Jake.'

'All right,' he said gently. 'You always did have a soft heart, Angelina. I remember the day we found that bird with the broken wing caught in the vines. You cried till your dad promised to take it to a vet.'

He was getting to her again. 'I only have a soft

heart for poor birds with broken wings,' she countered crisply. 'And poor people dying through no fault of their own. Not smooth-talking lawyers who go round trying to seduce old flames just for the heck of it.'

'Is that what you think I'm doing?'

'Come, now, Jake, you ran into me today by sheer accident. You haven't given me a second thought all these years.' Unlike herself. Even if she'd wanted to forget Jake, how could she when his eyes had been staring back at her on a daily basis for years? 'Your dear old friend Dorothy is buying a place up here,' she swept on. 'You spotted me again today, liked what you saw, and thought I'd be a convenient lay during your weekends up here.'

'That's a pretty harsh judgement.'

'I think it's a pretty honest one. Please don't try to con me, Jake. I won't like that. Be straight with me.'

'OK, you're right and you're wrong. I admit I haven't actively thought about you for years. But that doesn't mean I'd forgotten you. When I realised where I was going for lunch today, everything came flooding back. The way you made me feel that summer. The things that happened. I really wanted to see you again. I told myself it was just curiosity, or the wish to say sorry for being just a chump back then. But when I actually saw you, Angelina...when I saw you I—'

'Please don't say the world stopped,' she cut in drily.

He laughed. 'I won't. It actually sped up. At least, my pulse-rate did. Do you know how beautiful you are?' he said, his voice dropping low again. 'How sexy?'

Don't fall for all that bulldust. Keep your head, honey.

Angelina could almost hear those very words coming from Wilomena's mouth.

'You're not the first man to tell me that, Jake,' she said in a rather hard voice.

'I don't doubt it.'

'City men are amazingly inventive, especially when they're away from home. The Ambrosia Estate has become a popular venue for conferences,' she elaborated. 'Lots of them pass through all the time.'

'You sound as if you've been burnt a few times.'

'Who hasn't in this day and age?' came her off-hand reply. If he thought she'd jumped into bed with her fair share of such men, then all well and good. No way did she want him thinking he was the only man she'd ever known.

'I'm sorry but I really must go, Jake. I was in the middle of something important when you called. I'll see you on Saturday at the expo. I'm sure you can manage to find the right booth. Shall we say twelve-thirty?'

'Noon would be better.'

'Noon it is, then. Bye for now.' And she hung up.

Jake was grinning as he replaced his receiver.

Alex, old man, he thought elatedly, come next weekend, you're going to be history!

CHAPTER SEVEN

ANGELINA couldn't stop titivating herself. If she'd checked her make-up and hair once, she'd checked it a hundred times.

Not for the first time this morning, she hurried into the hotel bathroom so that she could stand in front of the cheval mirror that hung on the back of the door.

The dress she was wearing was not casual. But she knew she looked good in it, which was the most important thing to her right at that moment.

Light and silky, the sleeveless sheath skimmed her curvy figure, making her look slim yet shapely at the same time. Its scooped neckline stopped just short of showing any cleavage, the wide, softly frilled collar very feminine. The hem finished well above her knee on one side and dipped down almost to mid-calf on the other, as was the fashion this year. The print on the pale cream material was floral, the flowers small and well-spaced, their colours ranging from the palest pink to a deep plum, her favourite colour. She'd matched the dress with open-toed cream high heels and a plum handbag. Her lipstick and nail-polish were plum as well. Strong colours suited her, with her olive skin and dark hair and eyes.

Her hair—which had been up and down several

times so far this morning—was finally down, its natural wave and curl having been tamed somewhat
with a ruthless blowdrying, but it still kicked up on
the ends. Shoulder-blade-length, it was parted on one
side and looped behind her ears to show her gold and
pearl drops. A gold chain with a single gold and pearl
pendant adorned her neck. The floral scents of her
perfume, an extravagant one she'd bought during her
last shopping trip to Sydney, was only just detectable
on her skin. Angelina didn't like it when a woman's
perfume preceded her into a room like a tidal wave.

She stroked the figure-hugging dress down over
her hips before turning round and looking over her
shoulder at her back view. Her scowl soon became
a shrug. Nothing she could do about her Italian lower
half. She had wide hips and a big bottom, and that
was all there was to it.

Angelina turned back and looked with more approval at her front view. At least she had the breasts
to go with the backside. They were a definite plus.
Just as well, however, that her nipples were hidden
by the wideness of the collar, because she could feel
them now, pressing against the satiny confines of her
underwired bra, making her hotly aware of how excited she was. How incredibly, appallingly excited.

A small moan escaped her lips, Angelina stuffing
a closed fist into her mouth and biting on her knuck-
les in an effort to get some control over her silly self.
But she was fighting a losing battle. The truth was
she was dying to see Jake again. She wanted to see

that look in his eyes once more, the one which made her feel like the most beautiful girl in the world.

Oh, she knew that he'd probably looked at a hundred different girls that way over the years. There were no end of lovely-looking girls here in Sydney, model-slim girls with more sophistication and style than she had. But no matter. She could pretend she was the only one, just for one miserable lunch.

Surely there was no harm in that. Lunch was safe. They wouldn't really be alone. Impossible for him to get to her sexually during lunch, no matter what his secret agenda might be. Sharing a meal was also a good opportunity to find out more about him.

Her eyes went to her wrist-watch. It was ten-past ten, still almost two hours to go before noon. The minutes were dragging, but then, she'd been up since dawn.

She hadn't slept well, and she couldn't even blame the hotel bed. She hadn't slept well all week, her mind never giving her any peace. She'd been tormented by regrets and recriminations.

Of course, in hindsight, she *should* have told Jake about Alex straight away last Saturday when he'd come back to the restaurant. And she shouldn't have begun that silly charade, letting Jake think Alex was her boyfriend. No, not boyfriend. Lover. It had only made Jake even more determined, it seemed, to win her. She'd become a challenge.

By Friday her nerves had been so bad that she hadn't felt capable of driving down to Sydney, let alone coping with the inner-city traffic. Whenever she came down to visit Alex at weekends, she always stayed at the Rydges Hotel in North Sydney, which was near his school. There was never any need for her to drive over the Harbour Bridge. If she wanted to go shopping in the city during her weekend trips down, she caught the train over the bridge. She never attempted to drive. For a country-raised girl, driving in that congestion would be a nightmare.

But getting to the expo, and the Star City hotel, would require her to go over the bridge and negotiate all those confusing lanes that went off in myriad different directions. Her father had brought her down to a show at the Star City theatre last year, and even he'd taken a wrong turn. Much easier to catch the train down and get a cab from Central. Much easier to come down on the Friday, too, rather than wait till the Saturday morning.

Arnold had kindly driven her into the station yesterday morning and she'd arrived in Sydney just after two, giving her enough time after booking in at the hotel to go for a walk and locate where the weekend expo was being held. It was down on a nearby wharf, in a building that had once housed the old casino.

The finishing touches on the Ambrosia Estate booth were being made when she arrived and she'd been very impressed. It looked like a little piece of Italy, with vines climbing over a mock-pergola, from which hung big bunches of grapes—not real but very lifelike. The right side of the booth was dedicated to white wines, with the red wines on the left. Each side would have its own team of pretty female demonstrators for wine-tasting, she'd been informed by the man running the show. Cheese would be offered with the reds, slices of fruit with the drier whites, and exotic sweets with the dessert wines.

The only negative during her inspection tour was this man himself. He was a typical salesman. Thirtyish and suavely handsome with a moustache and goatee beard, he just couldn't help flirting with her. Not too strong for a first meeting. But Angelina had had plenty to do with salesmen at the resort, and she knew as sure as the sun was already up and shining that morning that today would be a different story. Today, he was going to come on much stronger. Today, he was going to be hands-on.

Which created a dilemma for Angelina. She didn't want to encourage the guy by turning up again today. At the same time, she didn't want Jake to think her presence wasn't required at the expo. She needed to actually be there at the booth, doing something constructive, when Jake showed up. Which meant she'd have to leave the sanctuary of her hotel room soon and make an appearance.

Angelina sighed. She hoped that Wayne—he must have told her his name ten times—didn't think she'd dolled herself up for him. Yesterday she'd only been wearing jeans and a simple white shirt, and he hadn't been able to stop eyeing her up and down.

The telephone suddenly ringing startled Angelina. As she hurried from the bathroom, she wondered who it would be. Unlikely to be Alex. The team wasn't allowed any outside calls during their weekend camp. The focus was to be all on swimming. Angelina had called him last night from the hotel and they'd talked for simply ages. Mostly about the expo. Alex was all for advertising their wines, unlike his grandfather, who'd been old-fashioned in his ways.

No, it couldn't be Alex, she thought as she crossed the hotel room and scooped up the receiver. Hopefully not the dreaded Wayne, wanting to know where she was.

'Yes?'

'Do you always answer the phone as if it's bad news?'

Jake. It was Jake. Angelina's stomach started to swirl.

'How did you know to ring me here?' she said.

'I was just talking to the chap running your booth at the expo and he mentioned you'd arrived yesterday. You yourself told me where you were staying, Angelina.'

'But what are you doing at the expo this early? You said noon. It's only just after ten.'

'I didn't want to risk not being able to find you later, so I thought I'd do a preliminary sortie. I'm glad I did. This place is a madhouse. You should see it. Which reminds me. Why aren't you down here, selling your wares? It wouldn't be because you don't really need to be here, would it? You couldn't possibly have lied to me about that too, the way you lied to me about when you would be arriving in Sydney?'

Angelina didn't know whether to be annoyed with

him, or charmed. 'I didn't want you pestering me any more than necessary.'

'Pestering! Wow, you really know how to take the wind out of a guy's sails, don't you?'

'Sorry. That was a bit harsh. But you know what I mean. Is there a purpose to this call, Jake, or is it just a softening-up trick?'

He laughed. 'I can see I'm going to have to be very careful with you.'

'Yes, you are. I'm fragile.'

He laughed again. 'You're about as fragile as Dorothy. OK, so I won't confess I just wanted to hear the sound of your voice. That would probably go down like a lead balloon. The second reason for this call is to check that you don't get seasick.'

'Seasick,' she repeated blankly. She was still thinking of his wanting to hear the sound of her voice.

'Yep, I'm planning on booking us a luncheon cruise on the harbour. That's another reason for my early arrival over here. I wanted to find out what was available.'

'Oh. Oh, how…lovely,' she finished, having almost said how romantic.

'I thought you might never have done that, living where you do.'

'No. No, I haven't. That's very thoughtful of you, Jake.'

'I cannot tell a lie. It wasn't thoughtful. It was my next best softening-up trick. After this phone call.'

Angelina smiled. 'You really are shameless.'

'And you really are beautiful. Yes, I know, I shouldn't have said that, either. I can't seem to help myself with you. My mouth has a mind of its own. Have you told Alex about us yet?'

'There is no *us*, Jake.'

'About lunch with me, then?'

'No.'

'You're only delaying the inevitable.'

'Yes. I know that.'

She heard his sharp intake of breath. 'Does that mean what I hope it means?'

'Let's just take one day at a time, Jake,' she said.

'Fair enough.'

'See you at the booth at noon,' she said, and hung up before she could say another single silly word.

CHAPTER EIGHT

JAKE watched her from a safe distance, Angelina totally unaware of his presence. He was a good thirty metres away from the Ambrosia Estate booth, with the milling crowds providing the perfect cover for his observation post.

She looked even more beautiful today than she had last Saturday. That dress was a stunner. But then, Angelina would look stunning in anything.

Woman was the right word to describe Angelina. So many girls these days were like stick insects. But not her. She was all soft curves and lush femininity. The two skinny blonde demonstrators working next to her in the booth looked positively anorexic by comparison.

Jake had been thinking about Angelina all week. She'd constantly distracted him at work and disturbed his sleep with dreams of the most erotic kind.

Last night had been especially erotic. He'd woken and reached for her in the bed—so real was the dream. But where he'd anticipated finding her warm and naked next to him, there'd only been a cold emptiness.

And to think she'd actually been *here*, in Sydney, last night, staying at the Star City hotel! This revelation had frustrated the hell out of him. If he'd known, he could have persuaded her to at least have dinner with him.

And she would have come. She'd virtually admitted to him over the phone this morning that she'd decided to give Alex the brush-off in favour of him.

Unfortunately, she'd also made it clear that he was still on probation. One day at a time, she'd said. He could not afford to rest on his laurels just yet. Or presume that she would say yes to more than a meal or two today.

Never in the last ten years had Jake had to be this patient with a woman. And never had he felt *less* patient.

His body was on fire, aching to be with her in the most basic way.

As his eyes roved over the silky dress she was wearing, his loins stirred alarmingly. He shifted away from the wall he was leaning against, taking several deep breaths and willing his flesh back to a semblance of control, and decency.

Suddenly, Angelina's eyes started to search the crowd as though she was looking for someone. Despite it only being ten to twelve, Jake instinctively knew she was looking for him. With rather anxious eyes, he thought. Perhaps because that Wayne fellow was being a pest. Ever since Jake had taken up his vantage point five minutes earlier, the sales rep had been chatting away to Angelina, his slimy dark eyes all over her.

When the sleazebag actually had the temerity to reach out and lay a hand on Angelina's bare arm,

Jake decided that waiting till noon was not on. He forged forward, amazed at the wave of fierce emotion which had consumed him.

Not jealousy. He didn't think for a moment Angelina fancied the guy. Jake had read her body language. He just couldn't bear for any man to touch her like that. Or to undress her with his eyes the way that guy had been doing.

The thought that *he'd* been doing some undressing with his own eyes was a sobering one. Though Jake quickly dismissed any guilt with the added thought that it was different with him. He *cared* about Angelina. It wasn't just a question of lust.

Her eyes lit up at the sight of him, making him feel almost ten feet tall.

'Ready to go, darling?' he said, firmly staking his claim.

Fortunately, Angelina didn't give him one of those don't-go-getting-carried-away-with-yourself looks she'd bestowed upon him last Saturday.

'I just have to get my handbag,' she replied eagerly.

Within thirty seconds, he was shepherding her away through the crowd, his hand resting possessively in the small of her back. Once they were out of sight of the booth, he rather expected her to tell him to keep his hands to himself.

But she didn't.

Angelina knew she was being foolish. But ooh...the touch of Jake's hand on her body was electric. His palm was like a hot iron, burning its way through her dress to her skin beneath. Heat radiated through her, making her feel as if she was glowing all over.

'Thank you for rescuing me from that creep,' she said as he steered her through the throng towards the exit.

'My pleasure.'

'I can't stand touchy-feely men.'

'Oops!' His hand promptly lifted away.

'Not you,' she hastily assured him with an upwards glance. 'I didn't mean you.'

Their eyes met and Angelina knew she'd just crossed a line, that line which she had taken such pains to draw earlier, but which was now in danger of disintegrating entirely.

Her eyes ran over him, and she thought how utterly gorgeous he was looking in his trendy city clothes. No jeans for him this time. But not a suit, either. His trousers were a bone colour, not dissimilar to the cream in her dress. Very expensive by the look of their cut, and the lack of creases. His shirt was made in black silk, worn open-necked, with its long sleeves rolled up to his elbows. Casual, yet sophisticated and suave, the epitome of the man about town, such a far cry from the Jake whom she'd ogled just as shamelessly sixteen years ago.

Only his eyes were the same. Still that same hard, icy blue, and still with the same intent. To get her into bed.

'That's a relief,' he said, and his hand settled right back where it had been.

A shiver ran down Angelina's spine. How would it feel if she had no clothes on at all? If she was lying with him, naked, in a bed, and he was sliding his hand down her back whilst the other was…?

She gulped the great lump which had formed in her throat and tried to find reasons for why his making love to her should never be allowed to happen. But none came to mind at that moment.

'Did that guy say or do anything really offensive?' Jake asked as he guided her out onto the wharf and into the sunshine. 'Do you want to me go back and sort him out?'

Angelina drew in some blessedly fresh air and tried to get herself back on to an even keel. 'Lord, no. No, that's not necessary. Wayne's harmless, really. Just too full of himself. And it's not as though I have to see him again.' Too late, she realised she'd made another blunder.

Jake pounced on it immediately. 'You don't have to go back to the booth today?'

'Not if I don't want to.'

'And do you want to?'

'Hardly.' Silly to say that she did. 'I thought I might do some shopping after our lunch,' she added, hoping to retrieve lost ground.

'Shopping for what?'

'Clothes.'

His gaze travelled slowly up and down her body. 'More clothes to drive men wild with lust?'

She flushed. 'That's not my intent when I buy a dress.'

'It might not be your intent,' he said drily. 'But the result's the same. I have to confess I do understand where poor Wayne was coming from. You'd tempt a saint, looking as you do today. And not many men are saints. But I doubt you'll have much time for shopping after our luncheon cruise. The one I've booked takes three hours. Most shops close at four on a Saturday. Besides, I was hoping you'd agree to come back to my place for a while. I live over in that direction there on MacMahon's Point,' he said, pointing straight across the expanse of sparkling blue water at the distant skyline of high-rise, harbour-hugging apartment blocks. 'I've already organised for the boat's captain to put in at the wharf there and let us off afterwards.'

'That was presumptuous of you, Jake,' came her surprisingly cool-sounding remark. Inside, she felt far from cool.

He shrugged. 'I didn't think you'd mind. I thought you might like to see where I live. I'm happy to drive you back to the hotel later in the afternoon. If you want to change for dinner, that is. But you look perfectly fine to go out with me exactly as you are.'

She laughed. 'You have today all planned out, don't you?'

'Being a lawyer has taught me that it's always wise to have a plan.'

'And do things always go according to your plans?'

'On the whole. But there are exceptions, of which

I suspect you might be one,' he finished with a rueful sigh.

She smiled, gratified that he thought she had more will-power and character than she actually possessed at that moment.

'You said one day at a time,' he reminded her. 'This is just one day, Angelina.'

He was right. It was. But she knew how Jake aimed for this day to end. All she could hope was that, when the time came, she had the courage to say no to him.

CHAPTER NINE

'YOU hear people saying how spectacular Sydney Harbour is,' Angelina said as they leant against the deck railing of the cruiser. 'I've admired it from afar many times. In movies and on television and from hotel-room windows. But it's not till you're on the water itself that you appreciate its beauty, and its size. Thank you so much for this experience, Jake.'

'I thought you might enjoy it.'

She truly had. Every bit of it. The views. The food. But especially the company.

Jake had to be one of the most intelligent and interesting men she'd ever talked to. Even if he wasn't drop-dead gorgeous and she hadn't been madly attracted to him, she'd have enjoyed his company these past three hours. They'd chatted about so many different topics, getting to know each other as the adults they'd become, not the teenagers they'd once been. She'd discovered they had similar tastes in books and movies, thrillers being their entertainment of choice. After agreeing to disagree on what kind of music was best, they'd argued happily about politics, discussed the world's leaders failing with peace and the environment, and in general had a great time, solving everything themselves with sweeping words of wisdom.

None of this would have been possible, Angelina realised, but for the other people on the cruise. Mostly tourists, with cameras which were whipped up at every opportunity to snap pictures of the bridge, the opera house and the shoreline. Their constant presence had allowed her to drop her defences and be more relaxed with Jake than she had been since he'd walked back into her life. It had been good to forget the threat of being seduced for a while and just enjoy Jake, the person, and not Jake, the sexual predator.

She was even beginning to reassess that judgement of him. Maybe she'd been harsh in thinking he was that shallow when it came to relationships. Just because he didn't want marriage and children didn't mean he wasn't capable of caring, in a fashion. Of course, his track record with women wasn't great. Even he'd admitted to that. But even men like Jake could change, couldn't they? Maybe he was getting to that age when he was ready for commitment.

But was he ready for a ready-made son, complete with mother attached?

Angelina felt that was too large a leap of faith.

No. Jake, the man, would still not be pleased when she finally told him the truth. Which was perhaps why she couldn't tell him yet. For one thing, she didn't want to spoil today. Surely she deserved one day of being totally selfish, of just being Angelina, the woman, not Angelina, the mother? It was so nice to be squired around by Jake, to have him lavish attention on her, to feel desired and wanted.

Of course, it was risky. But it was worth the risk to feel what she was feeling at the moment. Not in sixteen years had she experienced anything like it. This fizz of excitement dancing along her veins and through her head. Her very *light* head, she suddenly realised.

Her laugh sounded rather girlish, even to her own ears. 'I think I've had too much to drink.' The white wines served up with the buffet lunch had been excellent, and so easy to swallow.

'I'll make you some coffee when we get up to my place,' Jake offered. 'It's just a short walk from the wharf. Come on, this is where we get off.'

He hadn't lied about the shortness of the walk. But it was still far too long with her hand warmly encased within Jake's. By the time they'd strolled up the hill to his apartment block, and ridden up in the lift— alone together—to the fifteenth floor, Angelina was desperate to put some physical distance between them. She was glad when he dropped her hand to unlock and open his front door. But that was only a short respite. She needed longer.

'I—er—have to use your bathroom,' she said as soon as Jake shut the door behind them.

He gave her a sharp look, as though he knew exactly what she was doing. And why.

'This way,' he said crisply.

Her five-minute stay in the bathroom helped, although not the sight of the bathroom. How many people had bathrooms which had black marble right to the ceiling, not to mention real gold taps and corner spa baths big enough for two?

Angelina recalled that the living room—which she'd followed Jake across on her way to the bathroom—also had black marble tiles on the floor, not to mention thick white rugs, red leather furniture, sexy steel lamps and a television as big as a movie screen. Then there was the far wall, which was all glass, beyond which was a wide terrace and a view to die for.

The place had 'seduction palace' written all over it!

'This is a very expensive apartment, Jake,' she said when she finally joined him in the kitchen. It, too, had the same black marble on the bench-tops, and the latest in stainless-steel appliances. Above the double sinks was a wide window that overlooked the terrace and caught some more of the brilliant view of the harbour, and the bridge.

'It was all Edward's doing,' he said as he spooned the coffee into attractive stoneware mugs. 'He insisted I buy a flashy harbourside apartment with some of my inheritance.'

'Well...this is flashy all right.'

He looked up from his coffee-making, his expression disappointed. 'You don't like it.'

'No, no, I do. What's not to like? It's just... well...it does have ''bachelor pad'' written all over it.'

'True. But then that's what I am, Angelina. A

bachelor. I thought that was one of the things you liked about me. I fitted in with your priorities in life.'

She looked away before he glimpsed the truth on her face, walking over to slide open one of the glass doors that led out onto the balcony. 'Could we have our coffee outside?' she threw back at him, deliberately directing the conversation away from her priorities in life.

Jake shrugged. 'Whatever you fancy.'

Leading words, and one which Angelina struggled to ignore. If only he realised how much she fancied *him*. So far, she'd done a good job of keeping her desires hidden, but the fact she was even here, with him, alone, had to be telling.

She was standing against the glass security panels that bounded the terrace, her hands curled tightly over the top railing, when he joined her with the two steaming mugs.

'I remembered how you liked your coffee from last Saturday,' he said. 'I hope I got it right. Black, with one sugar?'

'Perfect,' she said, and went to take it from him. Stupidly, not with the handle. On contact with the red-hot stoneware, her hand automatically jerked back. At the same moment, Jake let the mug go and it crashed to the terrace, splintering apart on the terracotta tiles, some of the near-boiling black coffee splashing onto her stockinged legs.

Her cry of pain was real, Jake's reactions swift. Shoving his own mug onto a nearby table, he scooped Angelina up in his arms, and carried her with long strides back inside and over to the kitchen. There, he sat her on the marble counter, stripped off her shoes and swivelled her round to put her stockinged feet into the larger of the two sinks. Turning on the tap, he directed the cold water over her scalded legs.

'That water's freezing!' she cried out, and stamped her feet up and down in the sink.

'That's the idea,' he replied. 'It'll take the heat out of your skin and stop it from burning. Now, stop being such a baby.' And he kept swivelling the tap back and forth across her lower legs.

'You're getting my dress all wet,' she complained.

'I have a drier. Besides, there's coffee on that very pretty skirt, anyway. You'll have to take the dress off and soak it, if you don't want the whole thing to be ruined.'

Take her dress off! If she did that, then she'd be a goner for sure.

'Was this part of your plan for today? Spill hot coffee all over me so you could play knight the rescue and get my dress off at the same time?'

His blue eyes glittered with amusement. 'I'd love to say that I thought of it. In fact, I might put it away in my mental cupboard of plans for seducing difficult old flames. But given you dropped the mug, Angelina, might I ask you the same thing? Was this *your plan*,' he countered, his voice dropping to a low, sexy timbre, 'to spill coffee all over yourself so you could take off your dress in order to seduce *me*?'

If only he hadn't been so close, or his hands hadn't

been on her legs as well, or his eyes hadn't been searching hers.

'Could be,' she heard herself say in a faraway voice, her head whirling. But not with the wine this time. With desire. For him. 'Has it worked?' she murmured, her eyes drowning in his.

His hands stilled on her legs. Then slowly but surely, he turned off the tap and scooped her back up into his arms.

'Absolutely,' he said.

Jake's heart pounded as he carried her down the hallway towards the master bedroom.

This was the moment he'd been waiting and hoping for. There was no stopping him now.

Yet her eyes slightly bothered him. They seemed kind of dazed. Was she still tipsy from the wine she'd drunk over lunch? Surely not. She'd hadn't consumed that much.

He angled her through the bedroom door and carried her across the expanse of white shag carpet towards the king-sized bed with its gold satin quilt and matching pillows. Her calling the apartment flashy popped back into his mind. If she'd thought the rest of his place flashy, he wondered what she'd make of this room.

But she wasn't looking at the room. She was just looking at him. With those huge, liquid brown eyes of hers. Still dazed, they were. But also adoring.

Had there ever been a woman look at him quite like the way she was looking at him?

Only her, all those years ago, when she'd been just a girl. His heart flipped over at this realisation. Dear God, let him do this right this time, he thought, and laid her gently down across the bed.

She sucked in sharply when his hands slid up under the damp hem of her dress.

'Just taking your wet stockings off,' he explained softly, and made no attempt to do anything else as he peeled them off her and draped them over a nearby chair. Despite his own intense need, Jake knew instinctively not to go too fast. Or to do anything even remotely crude. Or aggressive.

Angelina was not like any other woman he'd known. She was different. Special. Fragile, she'd called herself this morning. He'd laughed at the time but he could see that she was right. She *was* fragile.

'Do you want me to take your dress off?' he asked. 'Or do you want to do that yourself?'

She just stared up at him for a few moments before rolling over and presenting her back to him.

The naivete behind this trusting gesture touched him, and reaffirmed his new assessment of her. His very first instinct about Angelina had been right after all. She might talk tough, but she wasn't tough. Or all that experienced, either. He suspected she hadn't had as many lovers as she'd implied. How could she have, with that eagle-eyed father of hers?

The thought made him even more determined to do this right.

The zipper on her dress was long, opening up the back right down to the swell of her buttocks. The sight of nothing but a thin white satin bra strap and the beginning of what looked like a matching thong did little for his resolve to take this as slowly as possible.

'Roll over,' he ordered a bit abruptly.

She did so, and those eyes were on him again. Wide now, and dilated. Her lips fell apart as her breathing quickened appreciably.

He tore his eyes away from hers and bent to ease the dress off her shoulders and draw it down her arms and over her hips, down her legs and off her feet. He tried to remain cool and in command, but the sight of her soft, curvy body—encased in sexy satin underwear—was unbearably exciting.

Hell, how *was* he going to control himself in the face of such temptation?

His hands were unsteady as he reached to unhook the front bra clip, hesitating for a moment before exposing her breasts to his increasingly lustful gaze.

They were as perfect as he'd known they'd be. Full and lush, with dusky-tipped aureoles and large, hard nipples seemingly begging to be sucked.

But he knew that would have to wait. If he started sucking her nipples now, he would become hopelessly lost in his own desires. Hers were the ones he wanted to satisfy this first time. His male ego demanded it. And something else, some part of him which he couldn't quite grasp yet.

'I have to sit you up for a sec,' he said, and did so with a gentle tug of her hands. The action had her breasts falling deliciously forward, twin orbs of erotic promise that he steadfastly ignored as he eased the bra off her body.

'You can lie back down,' he suggested as he moved over to put the bra on the chair with the dress and stockings.

She did, her face now flushed, her eyes still wide.

The decision to leave her with her G-string on was more for his composure than her comfort.

Her eyelashes flickered wildly when his hands went to the buttons of his shirt. Her lips fell further apart.

He undressed slowly, seemingly casual and confident in his actions, but inside he was going through hell. Never had a woman watched him so intently as he removed his clothes. There again, never had he done such a deliberate strip for a woman.

Jake knew he had a good body. Mostly God-given, but also because he looked after himself, having always worked out regularly. There was a gym and a swimming pool in the apartment complex which allowed him to keep fit nowadays with the minimum of effort. So he had no reason to be embarrassed once he was in the buff.

He had to confess that he could not recall being this turned on before. Yet he hadn't even kissed her.

Drawing on protection at that point was premature on Jake's usual standards, but it seemed a good idea to be prepared. Jake had an awful feeling that once he started any form of foreplay with Angelina, he would enter the danger zone. It proved strangely awkward, with her watching him with those almost awestruck eyes of hers.

He was relieved to join her on the bed, stretching out beside her and propping himself on one elbow so that he had one hand free. His right hand.

'Wait,' she whispered, and before he could stop her she wriggled out of her panties and tossed them away, her face flushed by the time she glanced back up at him.

He didn't dare look down there. Or to think about how much he wanted to slide over between her legs and just do it. Now. *Without* preliminaries. He ached to be inside her, to feel her hot wet flesh tight around him.

At least he could touch her there. And his free hand stroked down the centre of her body and slid between her legs.

Her moan echoed his own feelings. Already she was panting, her legs growing restless, her hips writhing as a woman's did when release was near. The selfish part of Jake wanted to stop so that he could be inside her. But experience warned him that things didn't always work out that way for a woman. Better he give her a climax this way first.

'Jake,' she cried out, her eyes dilated and desperate.

His mouth crashed down onto hers, smothering her cries as she came apart under his hand. He kissed her with a desperation of his own, his tongue echoing what he would rather be doing to her with his body. Its job done, his hand moved to play with her breasts, his still wet fingertips encircling her taut nipples. Jake kept kissing her, and playing with her nipples, elated when in no time her back began to arch away from the bed in that tell-tale way. Moaning, she clung to him, her left leg lifting up onto his hip, inviting him in.

Jake needed no further invitation, groaning as his flesh slid home to the hilt. The sensations as he pumped into her were a mixture of agony and ecstasy, for he could not possibly last very long. Yet he wanted to, wanted to feel her come again with him inside her.

Her muffled moans were encouraging, as were the movements of her body. She followed his rhythm, her hips rising with his forward surge and sinking back when he withdrew. He stopping kissing her and cupped her face instead, looking deep into her glazed eyes.

He didn't say a word, just concentrated on her, slowing his rhythm appreciably but going deeper with each stroke.

She gasped, then groaned.

'Good?' he asked.

She nodded, then grimaced.

He was in his stride now, no longer balancing on that dangerous edge, determined to make her come again. She drew in more sharply with each successive stroke, her mouth falling even wider apart. Her hands tightened around his back, her nails digging into his flesh.

He felt no pain, only pleasure. The pleasure of pleasing her.

Her climax was imminent. He could feel it, deep inside. The tightening. The quivering. The rush of heat that always preceded the first spasm.

'Jake. Oh, Jake,' she cried out, and then she was there. But so, astonishingly, was he. Instantly. Brilliantly.

Poets often spoke of stars exploding when two people in love made love. Jake always thought that was just so much crap.

But this time, it *was* not unlike stars exploding. His body trembled and his head did cartwheels. His mouth found hers again and he knew that this was where he wanted to be for the rest of his life. With her. No one else. Just Angelina. And he didn't mean living together, either. He wanted her as his life partner. His wife.

Angelina Winters. Till death them did part.

It didn't occur to Jake till much later, when he was lying quietly with her sleeping form in his arms, that Angelina might not be altogether cooperative in his achieving that goal.

'I might not want what you want, Jake,' she'd said to him earlier that day.

Jake thought about all she'd told him about herself so far. Her insistence that she was independent-minded career woman. Her claim to not want marriage and children.

And then he thought of her eyes today as he'd carried her into this bedroom.

Bulldust, he decided. All of that other stuff. Dorothy was right. Angelina had marriage and motherhood written all over her. She'd been burnt, that was all, by the wrong kind of man. Some sleazebag, probably. All it needed was the right kind of guy to come along, someone who really loved her.

'*Me!*' he pronounced out loud.

Jake still wasn't sure about becoming a father, but heck, he hadn't thought till now that he'd ever fall in love, or want to get married himself. But he did. And when Jake wanted something, he made it happen.

Angelina Mastroianni was going to be his wife, no matter what she thought she wanted. Because Jake knew what she really wanted. He'd seen it just now. And felt it. What he needed to do was make her feel it again. And again. And again. He had one weekend to cement his position in her life, and in her heart. Given that was a pretty short time span, Jake decided that the best way he could achieve that was through her body; her warm, luscious, possibly neglected body.

That pathetic boyfriend of hers hadn't been doing the right thing by Angelina. Jake was sure of it. Which was fine by him. It gave him an advantage.

Just thinking about making love to her again turned him on. Retrieving a condom from where he'd shoved a few under the pillows, he slipped it on, amazed but pleased to see that he was as hard as he'd been earlier, confirming his belief that this was a once-in-a-lifetime relationship.

Scooping her naked body back against him in the spoon position, he gently stroked her breasts till she stirred in his arms, then his hand slid slowly further down her body.

'Oh,' she gasped when his fingers started softly teasing the centre of her pleasure.

But there was nothing soft, or gentle, in Jake's mind. It was full of hard resolve, as hard as his desire-filled flesh.

As soon as she moaned, and began wriggling her bottom against him, he eased himself inside her from behind.

Angelina stiffened for a second, only to melt as soon as he started rocking back and forth inside her. She would never have conceived of making love like this, on their sides, with him pressed up against her back and his hands on her front, playing with her.

It was nothing like last time; that tender and romantic position where Jake had kissed her all the while and held her like a true lover. This was entirely different. This felt…decadent. Yet oh, so exciting.

Her head whirled as a wanton wildness overtook her.

'Harder, Jake,' she bit out in a voice she didn't recognise. 'Harder.'

He groaned, then increased his tempo.

'Yes,' she groaned, her body immediately rushing towards the abyss. 'Oh, yes. Yeesss!'

CHAPTER TEN

ANGELINA knew she was in trouble the next morning. Deep, deep trouble.

It was not long after sunrise, Jake was still fast asleep in the bedroom and she was curled up on the red leather sofa, her naked body wrapped in Jake's bathrobe, her hands cradling a not-too-hot mug of coffee, her eyes taking in the sun-drenched terrace, and the bridge beyond. The traffic on it was only light at this early hour, she noted.

But not for long. The day promised to be as bright and warm as yesterday.

Yesterday...

She took the mug away from her lips and sighed. Dear heaven, what had she done?

A small, dry laugh escaped her lips. What *hadn't* she done? more like it. Her behaviour in bed was bad enough, but it hadn't been confined to Jake's bed, had it? She'd been bad in the spa bath as well, and in the kitchen whilst he'd been microwaving them a meal. And here in this very room, on the rug, in front of the television.

It was as though Jake's making love to her that second time had released something in her, and suddenly she was hungry for it all. Every experience possible with Jake.

He hadn't minded, of course. Though she'd had the impression he was a bit surprised at one stage. Not with what she did. Perhaps he was just surprised that *she* would what she did, and with such avidness.

But as much as Angelina was worried sick by where this would all end, she could find no real regrets in her heart for the actual events of last night. How could you regret something that made you feel the way she felt this morning? Like a real woman for a change. A desired and desirable woman who had been made love to very, very well.

At least now she knew what Wilomena meant by having fun. It *had* been fun. At least, it had been with Jake. The man was the very devil with women all right. If she'd shocked him once, he'd shocked her a dozen times. Thrillingly, though.

The memories made her quiver with remembered pleasure.

'What are you doing up this early?'

Angelina almost spilt her coffee again, her whole body jumping at Jake's sudden appearance behind her.

As she glanced up over the back of the sofa at him, he bent to kiss her, one of his hands sliding down the front opening of the robe at the same time.

Angelina didn't know how she *didn't* spill the coffee this time.

'Mmm,' he murmured by the time he'd straightened. 'I know what I'm going to have for breakfast. Fancy a shower together?'

'Not till I've finished my coffee,' she replied with

creditable control, considering. Angelina had already decided that, whilst yesterday had been marvellous, today was another day entirely. Today, she had to start getting some control back over herself.

Watching Jake walk over to the nearby open-plan kitchen didn't exactly help that resolve, given that he was stark naked. She told herself not to look, but look she did. By the time he'd made his coffee and returned to sprawl in an adjacent chair, sipping his coffee with apparent nonchalance, her control was definitely at risk.

Gulping down the rest of her coffee, she uncurled her legs and made some excuse about seeing to her clothes, which Jake had actually popped into the washer and dryer at some stage last night. She was just hanging her fortunately crush-free dress on a coat hanger in the beautifully appointed laundry when Jake's arms went round her waist from behind.

'Methinks the lady is suffering morning-after syndrome,' he whispered as he started unsashing her robe.

'Not at all,' she lied coolly. 'I'm just a bit concerned about today, that's all. I really need to go over to the hotel this morning, change into some casual clothes and check out. Then I have to drop in at the expo and see how we're doing.' She really couldn't go home without knowing if this venture had been a success. Arnold would ask, and so would Alex.

'When's check-out time?' Jake asked, those busy hands of his not missing a beat as they drew erotic circles around her stiffening nipples.

Angelina swallowed. She really couldn't allow him to seduce her again so easily. But of course that was his talent, wasn't it? Seduction. And sex. Tender sex. Rough sex. Imaginative sex. Whatever was required. But still just sex. She had to remember she wasn't anything so special. Just more of a challenge than his usual chicky babe.

Or she *had* been.

'Ten-thirty,' she told him, swallowing again. Why didn't he stop that? On the other hand, why didn't *she* stop him? She was just so weak where he was concerned.

Was it love making her weak? Or could she take some comfort in hoping this was just sex for her as well? In a way, this made some sense. She'd lived a celibate life for so long that surely it was only natural that she'd go mad for sex, now that she'd discovered it. Maybe she wasn't madly in love with *him*, after all.

'We have plenty of time yet,' Jake said throatily, cupping her breasts and pulling her back hard against him.

She could feel his hardness through his bathrobe.

'I'll drive you over to the hotel around ten,' he murmured as he pulled the robe further open and nuzzled at her neck. 'And take you personally to the expo. Then we can go have lunch and do some shopping.'

'Shopping?' she echoed somewhat blankly, having reached that point when intelligent thought was nigh-on impossible.

'Didn't you say you wanted to go shopping?'

'Did I?' The robe slipped off one shoulder, then the other, before dropping to the floor. Suddenly, she felt more naked than she ever had been with him. And more vulnerable.

He was smiling when he turned her round in his arms.

'I dare say you've changed your mind, like a typical woman. But I have a fancy to buy you something really sexy to wear. Something…naughty.''

She stared up into his eyes, which were gleaming hotly down at her.

'You're still a very bad boy, aren't you, Jake?' she choked out.

'I haven't noticed you objecting,' he replied with a devilishly charming grin. 'Now, come have that shower with me, gorgeous.'

She went.

'Sydney really is a beautiful city,' Angelina said as they walked, hand in hand, through Hyde Park.

Jake glanced across at her, thinking how beautiful *she* looked today. Beautiful *and* sexy. Those jeans hugged her curvy body like a second skin. Too bad about that loose white shirt she was wearing over them. Though perhaps it was as well she wasn't wearing anything too revealing on top. Jake's possessiveness of her had increased overnight, along with his desire. He only had to touch her and he wanted to make love to her again.

Jake thought of what was in the plastic shopping

bag he was holding. The sexiest black corset he'd ever seen. Angelina had refused to try it on in the shop, but he knew there would be no such objections once he got her home.

'Sydney always looks great in the summer,' he agreed, very pleased with the way things were going.

'I guess the good weather is one of the reasons the expo has gone so well,' she remarked.

'Perhaps. But it always pays to have a good product. Your wines are going to be a big hit down here in Sydney, by the sound of things. Wayne was over the moon with the orders they'd already taken and the interest shown.'

'Men like Wayne are exaggerators,' Angelina said drily. 'But it does look promising.'

Jake had to admire the way Angelina's feet were firmly on the ground when it came to her business. She was no pushover, in lots of ways.

Sexually, however, she was putty in his hands. Jake couldn't wait to get her alone again.

'I work not far from here,' he pointed out. 'My office is in that tall bluish building over there. If the sun's out, I come over to the park and eat my lunch here. Right here, in fact.' And he pulled her down onto a seat under a huge tree that provided almost an acre of shade.

His arm wound round her shoulders and his lips pressed into her hair. 'Want to make out?' he whispered.

'Jake Winters, behave yourself. I don't think we

need to make out in public, do you? We've been at it like rabbits. A breather is definitely called for.'

'Not rabbits,' he said. '*Lovers*. Once is never enough for lovers.'

'Once! How about one times twenty? I didn't know it was possible to have so much sex in one weekend.'

'Amazing, isn't it?'

Angelina glanced up into Jake's grinning face and took a mental photo of it for her memory bank. He looked so handsome today. And so happy.

She doubted he'd look quite so happy once he found out about Alex.

'What?' he said, his grin fading.

It constantly surprised Angelina, the way he seemed to pick up on her inner feelings, without her having to say a word. It was almost as though he could read her mind sometimes. He certainly knew whenever she wanted him again.

Unfortunately, this was almost continuously. She simply could not get enough of him. Even now, she wanted him to take her home. She wanted him to strip her off and lace her into that decadent-looking corset and do whatever it was he had in mind to do to her whilst she was wearing it.

Hopefully, he couldn't read her thoughts. She seriously needed this breather so she could think.

'What is it?' he repeated. 'Tell me true.'

'Nothing much. I was thinking how handsome you were. And how much I like you with short hair.'

'And I like you with long.'

She flushed as she thought of what he had done with her hair on one occasion last night. He really was a wicked man.

No, not truly wicked, Angelina conceded. But seriously naughty. A very good lover, though. Very knowledgeable about women's bodies, and totally uninhibited when it came to using that knowledge. How on earth was she going to find the strength to tell Jake about Alex, when it meant she would have to give up his lovemaking?

Because it was all going to end once the truth came out. If there was one thing the last twenty-four hours had proved to Angelina, it was that Jake only had one need for a woman, and that was as his sexual partner. His plaything. Even his calling her his lover just now was telling. Why not girlfriend? Lover had that for-sex-only connotation about it.

No, Jake hadn't changed in that regard. His aim had been to sleep with her. And now that he had, any complications would have him running a mile.

And Alex, let's face it, she thought, was one big complication.

'What a shame today has to end,' she said with a sigh.

'Does it have to?'

'Time marches on. Nothing can change that.'

'You could always stay the night with me, go home tomorrow.'

She was seriously tempted. If she'd been in bed

with him at this moment, with his hands on her naked body, she probably would have said yes.

'Sorry,' she said crisply. 'No can do. I have to get back home tonight. Work tomorrow.'

'Yeah. Same here. I'm due in court first thing in the morning.'

'On that case you told me about?' Angelina asked, grateful for the opportunity to get her mind off sex. 'The lady who's dying of lung cancer?'

'That's the one. I have to deliver my closing address.'

'Are you ready?'

'I should hope so. I've been living and breathing that case for months.'

'Do you memorise your speeches?'

'Not really. I do write my ideas down. But I never try to remember them word for word. That's the sure way to go blank and stuff it up. No, I prepare well and then I talk from the heart. You do make the occasional stumble over words that way, but the jury never minds that, if they know you're being sincere.'

'I hope you win,' she said with feeling.

'Don't worry,' Jake returned with a little squeeze of her shoulders. 'We will.'

Angelina abruptly jumped to her feet. 'Come on, let's walk some more. I want to go see St Mary's Cathedral.' And she yanked a groaning Jake to his feet.

'More walking? Can't we just sit here and cuddle?'

'You've had more than enough cuddling for one weekend. *Up!*'

'Wow. I like it when you're bossy. Would you like to be on top when we get back to my place?'

'Get that bag and come on!' She was already off, walking in the direction of the cathedral, not giving him the opportunity to take her hand again.

'Oh, look!' she exclaimed when they emerged from the park directly across from the main cathedral steps. 'There's a wedding car just arriving. Let's go over and watch, Jake. I love watching weddings.' Anything but going back to his place yet.

'Why?'

'Because!'

'That's no reason from a girl who says she doesn't want to get married.'

'I don't want to be an astronaut, either,' she argued, 'but I like watching their exploits.'

'I suppose you could compare marriage to flying into space.'

'It's certainly a risky venture.'

'But risk can be exciting.'

Angelina arched her eyebrows. 'This, from a man who said *he* never wanted to get married?'

'Maybe I've changed my mind.'

Jake saw the shock reverberate in her eyes. 'You... you don't mean that,' she said stiffly.

Jake immediately regretted his possibly ill-judged words. If he rushed her, he might lose what he wanted most. After all, this was just their first weekend together. Best stick to sex for now.

'Never say never about anything,' he remarked nonchalantly. 'That's my motto.'

'For the record, I never actually said I would *never* get married. I just said it wasn't a priority of mine.'

Jake felt heartened by the carefulness in her wording.

'That's good,' he said with a smile. 'I like a girl who keeps her options open.''

Her hitting him playfully on the arm broke the tension he'd foolishly created.

'I'm just a sex object to you, aren't I?' she accused.

'Absolutely. So, do you want to go look at this wedding, or do you want to go home? Don't forget, we've only got four hours before I drive you home. We'll have to set off by eight if I want to be back in Sydney by midnight. I'm a Cinderella kind of guy when I have to be in court in the morning.'

'Decisions. Decisions.'

'Yeah, life's a bitch, isn't it? So what do you reckon? Which is it to be?'

Angelina knew he thought she'd opt to go home. And she wanted to. She wanted to so much it was criminal.

All the more reason not to.

'I think it would do you good to see that there is more to a relationship than just sex. That couple in there are about to promise to love and cherish each other till death them do part.'

'Until divorce them do part, don't you mean?'

'You're a cynic, do you know that?'

'Takes one to know one.'

'Point taken. But I still want to see the wedding,' she said firmly, and walked over to press the button that would change the traffic lights. 'Despite the fact that the bride has already gone inside.'

'Fine by me. I not only like to watch sometimes, but also to wait. Waiting whets the appetite further.'

'You have a one-track mind.'

'Where you're concerned, I have.'

'You'd better behave yourself in this church.'

'I'll be an angel.'

'Don't be facetious.'

The lights changed and Angelina launched herself across the road, Jake hot on her heels. She could hear the organ blaring out the *Wedding March* even from that distance.

'No wandering hands during the ceremony,' she warned him as they skipped up the steps.

'Definitely not. I know you. You won't be able to control yourself.''

'I will!' she countered, but blushingly.

'No? Pity. Well, let's hope this isn't one of those long ceremonies. I'm not sure I'll be able to sit on a hard pew for more than twenty minutes, max.''

She laughed, not a good idea since they'd just entered the vaulted interior of the cathedral, right at the moment when the organ stopped. Her laughter echoed up into the cavernous and unfortunately silent ceiling. Several heads whipped round to glare.

'Sorry,' Jake apologised to them. 'I can't take her anywhere.'

'Stop it,' Angelina hissed. 'Just shut up and watch.'

He shut up. But not for long.

'Hard to see much from this far back. Want to get closer?'

'No! I can't trust you to behave.'

'True. I've always been a bad boy in churches. Can't stand all the hush-hush nonsense. Makes me want to break out.'

'If you embarrass me,' she whispered, 'I won't go to your place with you afterwards at all. I'll make you drive me straight home to the Hunter Valley.'

'Don't think so,' he returned just as softly. 'You left that pretty handbag behind, remember? We'll have to go collect it. Although, perhaps not. You could always collect it next weekend.'

Angelique frowned. She'd been trying not to think about tomorrow, let alone next weekend. 'I...I have to have lunch with Alex next weekend.'

'You don't *have* to do anything of the kind. Call him. Tell him it's over by phone.'

'No.'

'I knew you'd say that,' he muttered. 'OK, go to lunch with him if you have to. But that's just on the Saturday during the day. As soon as you're finished with him...*permanently* this time...I will expect you at my place. Shall we say four? Five?'

'Make it six.' The swimming carnival wouldn't finish till five.

'That's one hell of a long lunch. I sure hope it's

going to be somewhere public. All right, all right, so I'm acting like a jealous fool. Six, it is. I'll book us a table for dinner at eight. You can stay over till Sunday night, can't you?'

Angelina swallowed. She really shouldn't let this fiasco continue. It wasn't right. She should tell him the truth.

But she just couldn't.

'All right,' she said with a sigh. 'Now hush up.'

He hushed up, but a small boy several rows up from them didn't. He started whinging and whining about wanting to go outside. Several warnings from both his parents to be quiet and to sit still had no effect. Finally, the father lost his patience, swooped the child up in his arms and headed with swift strides back down the aisle, past Angelina and Jake.

Angelina smiled a wry smile. She remembered full well the trials and tribulations of taking a small boy to church.

Jake's suddenly leaping to his feet startled her. 'Be back in a minute,' he said. 'Got to check on something.' And he was off, bolting down the aisle after the man and child.

Angelina jumped up as well, and hurried after the three of them, catching up with Jake on the cathedral steps. He was standing there, staring, an odd confusion in his eyes.

Her hand on his tensely held arm was gentle. 'You see?' she said quietly as her gaze followed Jake's to where the father was happily lighting up a cigarette whilst he watched his son enjoying himself immensely jumping up and down the steps. 'No need to worry.'

'I thought…'

'Yes, I know what you thought,' she said softly.

She actually felt the shudder run all through Jake.

'Can we get away from here?' he said, glancing around at all the onlookers who were gathering to see the bride emerge.

'All right.' She tucked her arm through his and they just walked in silence for a while, finding their way across the road and back into the park at the next intersection.

'Is that what your father did to you, Jake?' she asked gently at last. 'Hit you?'

'No, not my father. I never knew my father. He did a flit before I was born. It was my mother who did the honours. Man, she had a punch on her, that woman. Not a day went by that she didn't lay into me for some reason. Just about anything would set her off, especially when she'd been drinking. Sometimes it was just the way I looked at her. I can still remember how scared I was to go home after school, right from the time I was in kindergarten. Although weekends were the worst. No school to escape to those days.'

Angelina was both horrified and saddened by his story. What kind of a mother would do that to her son? 'But didn't the teachers notice?' she asked. 'I mean…there must have been bruises.'

He shrugged. 'I'm a boy. Boys get bruises all the time. If they did notice, they just looked the other way. Teachers weren't always as conscientious in reporting such matters back then as they are now.'

'But what about you grandparents? Your aunts and uncles? Neighbours? Wasn't there anyone who cared?'

'Not that I knew of. Mum was estranged from her family. And the neighbours we had were just as bad. It was not a salubrious street.'

'So what happened in the end? Did you run away?'

'I put up with it as long as I could. By the time I was in high school, I didn't go home much so I didn't get hit as often. I spent more and more time on the streets after school. Got into a gang. God knows how I didn't get arrested for shoplifting. I thought I was smart but I was just lucky. Anyway, one day when I was around fifteen, I came home late and Mum started swinging at me with this frying pan. Great heavy thing it was. Collected me a beauty. I'm not sure what happened next but it was Mum who ended up on the floor. Made me feel sick afterwards, I can tell you. But then…aggression breeds aggression. That was when I walked out and never went back.'

'But where did you live?'

'On the streets, of course.'

'But…'

'Look, I survived, OK, thanks to Edward and Dorothy. Let's not get into this. It's all dead and gone, even the lady herself. I looked her up last year when Edward died and found out she'd passed away years ago. Hepatitis. I didn't grieve, but I needed to know what had happened to her. Closure, I guess.'

Closure? The man who'd started shaking at the sight of a father showing even a small amount of impatience with his son was a long way from closure. Angelina was so glad that she had never used corporal punishment on her son. She'd never allowed her father to hit Alex either, no matter what.

Poor Jake. All of a sudden, she wanted to hold him and love him, to make up to him for everything he'd suffered as a child.

'Let's go home, Jake,' she suggested softly.

He stopped walking to throw her a speculative glance. 'Home, as in your home or my home?'

'Your home.'

'Now you're talking.'

But she didn't do much talking on the way home. She kept thinking of everything Jake had suffered as a child.

It explained why he didn't want to have children himself. Clearly, he was afraid he'd be a bad father, that the cycle of physical abuse would continue. Angelina didn't believe that it would for a moment. Not with Jake.

Still, it was what Jake thought that counted.

It was going to come as a terrible shock when she told him about Alex. Perhaps it was as well, Angelina realised, that their son was a teenager and not a baby.

'You've gone rather quiet,' Jake said as he unlocked his front door and ushered her inside. 'Is something wrong?'

'Wrong? No, no, nothing wrong.'

'It's Alex, isn't it? You're worried about him.'

'Alex will be fine,' she said. And he would be, too. He was going to be thrilled to have a father like Jake. It was Jake's reaction that worried her.

'So what is it?'

'I'm worried that I might be getting addicted to this.'

'To what?'

'To being with you.'

He dropped the shopping bag, kicked the door shut behind them and drew her into his arms once more. 'There are worse addictions, you know,' he murmured as he bent his mouth to hers.

Angelina wasn't so sure. Already it was responsible for her changing her mind about telling Jake the truth. And possibly for longer than a couple of weekends.

'This is one addiction which I would happily subscribe to,' Jake muttered against her lips. 'Come on, gorgeous,' he said, taking her hand and scooping up the shopping bag at the same time. 'Your breather is up.'

CHAPTER ELEVEN

'THURSDAY,' Angelina muttered to herself as she set about making her bed.

Four days since she'd seen Jake. Four long, boring, lonely days. And two more till she saw him again.

Coming round to the other side of her double bed, she picked up the pillow on that side and held it against her cheek. This was where Jake had laid his head the other night.

Could she still smell the scent of him on it?

Angelina imagined she could.

It had been quite late by the time Jake had driven her home last Sunday. She hadn't thought he would want to come in with her; hadn't anticipated it. But he'd insisted on walking her to the door, then claimed he needed to come inside to use the bathroom before driving back.

Her panic had been instant, and intense. For how could she let him come in? The place was full of Alex memorabilia. Photos everywhere. Trophies in his bedroom. Stuff on the fridge.

She'd finally managed to stall Jake at the door, saying that the place was a mess and she'd die of embarrassment if he saw it like that.

'Just give me one minute,' she'd begged. 'Please, Jake.'

He'd seemed amused. 'Don't tell me you're not perfect,' he'd said.

'Hardly,' she'd replied. 'Who is?'

Her dash around the rooms had been like something out of a farce. She'd scooped all the photos on top of the sideboard into the top drawer. The same with the ones on her bedside chests. She almost missed the reminder for Alex's swimming carnival on the fridge door, shoving it on top, along with the magnet photo of him as a baby. Alex's bedroom was a lost cause so she just closed that door, then flung open the bathroom door so that Jake wouldn't walk into his son's room by mistake.

He hadn't. But neither had he left after his trip to the bathroom, as she'd expected him to. He'd kissed her again, and soon she was ripping at his shirt and pulling him into her bedroom—the two-hour drive enclosed in that sexy car with Jake had done dreadful things to her resolve to be good—and the last thing Angelina remembered was falling asleep in his arms.

When she'd woken in the morning he was gone.

Mid-morning that Monday, a huge arrangement of red roses had arrived, with a card attached saying, 'Next weekend can't come quickly enough. Jake.'

The flowers were still alive and utterly gorgeous, sitting on the sideboard in place of the still absent photos. She didn't dare put any of them back up yet. In fact, since last Sunday, she'd locked Alex's bedroom door, and hidden anything else that might give the game away if Jake ever showed up here again. After his phone call last night, Angelina wouldn't be at all surprised at his driving up tonight. He'd been so excited after winning that case.

And missing her terribly, he'd said.

Angelina sighed. He wasn't the only one.

Jake sat down on his favourite seat in Hyde Park, placed the banana smoothie on the grass at his feet, then proceeded to unwrap his king-sized roll. This was the first time he'd had the opportunity to eat lunch in the park this week. Not because of the weather. Sydney had continued to be dry and warm. Circumstance had been the guilty party.

Monday, he'd been too wrecked to eat lunch. He'd had to call on every reserve of strength he had to deliver his closing address in court that morning, the weekend finally catching up with him. After the jury had retired to consider their verdict, he'd gone home and just collapsed into bed. Tuesday, he'd been far too agitated to eat. The jury had still been out. Wednesday, he'd been much too elated. At eleven that morning, the jury had found for the plaintiff to the tune of fourteen million dollars.

Now it was Thursday and the bedlam of the last couple of days was hopefully behind him. If another television station showed at his office, wanting another damned interview, he was going to go bush, preferably to the Hunter Valley.

Jake loved being a litigator. Loved having victories over the bad guys. Attention from the media, however, was not one of his loves. He hated having cameras and microphones shoved in his face. Of course, the law firm he worked for didn't mind one bit. But that kind of publicity was not Jake's bag, even if it did result in his being offered a partnership.

Strangely, Jake wasn't sure if he wanted to become a partner in Keats, Marsden and Johnson. Neither did he fancy being pushed into taking on the inevitable rush of perhaps not-so-worthy clients who thought they could make a mint out of suing their bosses over supposedly adverse working conditions. He'd only won this case because his client had a genuine complaint. Copycat cases rarely had the same integrity, or sympathy.

Jake munched into his salmon and salad roll—man, it tasted good—and wondered if now was the right time for him to make a move, start up a practice of his own. He'd be free then to take on only the clients he really wanted to represent. He wouldn't be influenced by money, which a big law firm invariably was. Of course, this would mean forgoing his six-figure salary plus bonuses, not to mention his generous expense account. It would also mean a lot of work. Starting up your own business involved a lot of red tape.

On the plus side, he would be his own boss. And the temporary loss of salary wouldn't be any great hardship. He still had a small fortune in cash left over from Edward's legacy.

Maybe he'd run the idea by Angelina tonight. She

was a businesswoman. She would know what was involved. See what she thought.

Aah, Angelina…

Already, he was looking forward to talking to her tonight. Their nightly chat was the highlight of his day, something to look forward to after work. He would ring her a lot more than that, but Angelina had forbidden him to call during the day, claiming she'd never get anything done if he did that.

Possibly true. Once they were on the phone together, they sometimes talked for hours.

Of course, he *had* broken the rules and called her as soon as the verdict came in on the Wednesday. But that was a special occasion and he hadn't kept her on the line for long.

The salad and salmon roll duly disposed of, Jake picked up his banana smoothie and started to sip.

How soon, he wondered, could he tell her he loved her and wanted to marry her?

Not too soon, Jake suspected.

A couple of times last weekend, she'd fallen silent on him. Suspiciously silent. You could almost hear the wheels turning away in her brain. Yet she'd been unforthcoming when he'd asked her what was wrong.

In a way, she was secretive. She rarely opened up to him about herself in any depth. And she never talked about her feelings for him.

In the past, he hadn't been able to stop women telling him their feelings, especially how much they loved him. Angelina never went near the subject of love. She said flattering things about his lovemaking but that wasn't the same.

Already addicted to having sex with him, she'd said last Sunday.

Jake frowned. He didn't like the idea that she might be only coming back to see him this weekend for more of the same. There was no doubting she liked sex. After his initially thinking she was pretty inexperienced in bed, she'd turned into a veritable tiger.

Once his mind took that tack, the worry started up that she hadn't been totally truthful over what she was up to this coming Saturday. To put aside a whole day to tell any man she was breaking up with him seemed excessively kind.

Maybe she's not going to break up with him at all, a dark voice whispered in his head. Maybe she's going to spend the whole day at Alex's place, in Alex's bed. And then come on to *his* bed for the rest of the weekend.

The idea revolted him. But it was possible, wasn't it? She had a very high sex drive. But was she capable of that level of deception?

He wouldn't have thought so. Still, his buying that huge diamond engagement ring yesterday afternoon now struck him as being ridiculously premature. Amazing the things a man in love would do! Fools did rush in, as the saying went.

The buzzing on Jake's cellphone had him sitting up abruptly, his banana smoothie slurping back and forth in its cardboard carton. Setting the drink down, he fished his phone out of his trouser pocket, clicked it on and swept it up to his ear.

'Yes?'

'Sally here, Jake. Sorry to bother you, but if you've finished your lunch perhaps you should get back here. You have a visitor.'

'A visitor. What kind of visitor?'

'A young man. Name of Alex.'

Alex! Jake didn't have any colleagues or acquaintances named Alex, so presumably this had to be *the* Alex.

Jake frowned over Sally calling him young. Of course, Sally thought anyone under forty was young, but it sounded as though Angelina's Alex was what was commonly called a 'younger' man.

Jake tried to ignore the instant stab of jealousy and focus on what the fool was doing, showing up at *his* office.

All he could think of was that Angelina had changed her mind and broken up with Alex over the phone, plus told him the identity of the guy she'd thrown him over for.

Jake groaned. As much as he was happy to find that his paranoid thoughts about Angelina two-timing him were just that…paranoid, the last thing he wanted was a confrontation with a furious ex boyfriend.

'I gather you know who I'm talking about,' Sally said.

'Possibly. Does my visitor have a second name?'

'Mastroianni,' Sally supplied.

'*Mastroianni!*' he repeated, totally taken aback.

And then the penny dropped. Alex was some kind of relative. Angelina had said he was half-Italian. Maybe that was what she'd meant about her relationship with him being complicated. If he was a cousin or something, she would have to explain things more fully. She couldn't just dump the guy without giving him a reason.

'I think you should get back here, Jake. This is something you have to attend to personally, by the look of things.'

'OK,' Jake said with a sigh. 'Tell him I'll be there shortly.'

The offices of Keats, Marsden and Johnson were spacious and classy, occupying half of the tenth floor of the building Jake had pointed out to Angelina the previous Sunday. Their main reception area was set directly opposite the lift well, behind a solid glass wall and two equally solid glass doors. Sally reigned over the reception desk and the waiting room, and had done so for many years. Although not unattractive for her age—she had turned fifty last month—Sally was the exception to the rule that highly visible Sydney receptionists should be curvy blondes with seductive smiles.

Jake, for one, enjoyed the wonderfully pragmatic and no-nonsense atmosphere Sally brought to the firm. Actually, Sally was one of the reasons he just might stay. He'd miss her if he left.

'Well?' he said as he strode in. 'Where is he and what am I in for?'

Sally glanced up, her no-nonsense grey eyes sweeping over him from top to toe in a critical survey, as though she were meeting him for the first time. Jake found himself automatically straightening his tie and wondering if his fly was undone.

'A shock, I would think,' she said drily. 'I put him in your office to wait for you.'

Jake ground to a halt beside her desk. 'What did you do that for? And what kind of a shock? Don't tell me he's a big bruiser.'

'He's not small,' she said, her grey eyes now gleaming rather mischievously. 'But then, neither are you.'

Jake wasn't sure if he was getting the subtle meaning behind this interchange.

'Looking for a fight, is he?'

'I wouldn't think so. More likely some answers to some questions.'

'Do you know something here that I don't know?'

Her finely plucked eyebrows lifted in feigned innocence. 'Know? No, I don't *know* anything. But I am a highly observant person, and a darned good guesser.'

'Sally, remind me to have you fired when I get to be partner.'

'Aah, so you've changed your mind about going out on your own, have you?'

He just stared at her. The woman had to be a witch in disguise. He had never discussed that idea with anyone in this firm.

'How did...? No, no, I am not going to ask.'

'Like I said,' she threw after him as he strode off down the corridor towards his office, 'I'm a darned good guesser.'

Jake hesitated at his door, irritating himself when he started checking his clothes again, as if he was going in for a bloody interview. Comforted that he looked his best in one of his newest business suits— the charcoal-grey mohair-blend—Jake still slicked his unslickably short hair back from his face before reaching for the knob.

'Sorry to keep you waiting,' he ground out as he opened the door and walked in.

The only other occupant of Jake's office immediately spun round from where he'd been standing at the corner window.

He was tall, though not as tall as Jake, or as solidly built. He was very good-looking, with strong facial features and an elegantly athletic frame. His long-lashed blue eyes reminded Jake of someone, but Jake couldn't remember who. His hair, which was dark and thick, was cut very short. Short was the fashion at the moment.

The only thing wrong with Jake's visitor was that he was dressed in a school uniform.

A shock, Sally had said.

She'd been right there.

This *couldn't* be the Alex Angelina had talked about. As sexy as Angelina was, he couldn't see her in the role of conscienceless cradle-snatcher. This boy could not be a day over seventeen. Eighteen, at a pinch.

Then who was he? Her ex-lover's younger brother? His son, maybe? Alex Mastroianni junior? If so, what was he doing here? And why was he staring at *him* as if he'd seen a bloody ghost or something?

Certainly, he wasn't in the mood for this!

'You wanted to see me?' he said abruptly, and continued round behind his desk, which sat adjacent to the window. 'Sit down,' he said with a gesture towards the two upright chairs that faced his desk. Then sat down himself.

The boy just stood there, staring.

Jake sighed.

'I gather your name is Alex Mastroianni,' he said. 'I'm Jake Winters.'

'Yes, I know,' the boy said, finding his voice at last. 'I saw you on the news last night. Twice. First on Channel Nine. Then later on Channel Two.'

'Aah yes, the news. We haven't met before, have we?' he asked, his mind teasing him again with that vague sense of recognition.

'No. Never,' the boy said.

'So what can I do for you, Mr Mastroianni?'

Jake decided to play this straight, as though the teenager before him was a potential client, and his name just a weird coincidence, which it very well might be. Life was sometimes stranger than fiction.

'Are you in need of a lawyer?'

The boy smiled. And again, reminded him of someone.

'Please call me Alex,' he said with a cool assurance that surprised Jake. Having found his tongue, he seemed to have found a degree of confidence as well.

'Very well. Alex. Please, do sit down. You're making me nervous, standing over there.'

The boy laughed. 'Not as nervous as I am.'

But he did sit down.

'You don't look nervous,' Jake said.

'Yeah, well, trust me, I am.'

'You don't have to be nervous with me. You can tell me anything. There is such a thing as client-lawyer privilege. I can't divulge anything you tell me. Like a priest.'

The boy just sat there a while longer, looking at him a bit like Sally had looked at him earlier, as though he was trying to see something in his face, or perhaps in his eyes. Was he wondering if he could be trusted?

Jake decided not to press. He didn't have any appointments for a while. He had the time to be patient, and, quite frankly, he was curious. Very curious.

'Do you remember a girl named Angelina Mastroianni?' the boy asked after a minute or two of tension-making silence. 'In case you've forgotten, you picked grapes at her father's vineyard in the Hunter Valley sixteen years ago.'

Jake snapped forward in his chair, his hands reaching for the nearest object. A Biro. He gripped it tightly and prayed this kid wasn't going to say something he didn't want to hear.

'I remember,' he returned tautly as his fingers

tightened. 'So what is Angelina to you? A cousin? An aunt?'

Stupid question, that last one, Jake. Angelina doesn't have any brothers or sisters so how could she be an aunt?

'No,' the boy denied. 'Nothing like that.'

Nothing like that. Then what?

'She's my mother.'

The Biro snapped. Clean in two.

'Your mother,' Jake repeated in a numb voice.

'Yes.'

'That's impossible! Angelina isn't old enough to be your mother!' He knew for a fact that sixteen years ago, she'd been a virgin. One and one did not make two here.

'I look old for my age. I'm only fifteen. I don't turn sixteen till the twenty-fourth of November this year.'

Jake's mind reeled. Only fifteen. And his birthday was in late November. He quickly counted backwards and landed on late February as the date of his conception. If Jake had been reeling before, he now went into serious shock.

It wasn't possible. He'd pulled out that night. Sort of. Well, maybe not in time. OK, so it *was* possible. But just as possible that Angelina had gone from him to some other guy. These things did happen once a girl had lost her virginity.

His gaze raked over the handsome boy sitting before him as he tried to work out all that Angelina had told him since they'd met up again. The lies.

No, not lies. But definitely verbal sleight of hand.

She'd deliberately kept Alex's true identity secret from him, and the question was why? It wasn't as though single mothers were uncommon these days. Even Italian ones.

'And your father?'

Even as he croaked out the question, Jake saw the truth staring back at him. Those eyes. They were *his*. So was the chin. And the hairline. Even the ears.

'Why, it's you, of course, Mr Winters,' the boy said with some bemusement in his voice, as though he was surprised Jake hadn't realised already. '*You're* my father.'

CHAPTER TWELVE

ANGELINA was behind the reception desk, booking in the Williams family, when Jake's yellow Ferrari shot down the driveway and braked to an abrupt halt under the covered archway on the other side of Mr Williams's sedate navy sedan.

Her heart began to thud.

So Jake had decided he couldn't wait till the weekend, either!

'Wow!' Mr Williams exclaimed. 'I've always wanted to cruise around Australia in a car like that.'

'In your dreams, darling,' his wife said. 'Where would we put the kids for starters?'

'With your mother, preferably,' he quipped back.

Jake, Angelina noted, did not get out of the car and come inside. Instead, after glancing over his shoulder at the reception area—which was clearly visible through the mainly glass front wall—he just sat, drumming his fingers on the steering wheel. Waiting, obviously, till she was alone.

A swirling sensation began to eddy in Angelina's stomach. But she didn't let her excitement show.

'Here are the keys to your suite,' she said with a smile as she handed them over. 'If you follow the driveway round the back, you can park right outside your main door. The pool is heated and open till ten.

The tennis court is available till the same time. Dinner starts at six in the restaurant. Did you see the restaurant as you drove in?'

'Sure did. Looks fabulous,' the wife gushed.

'Breakfast is in the same place from six-thirty till nine-thirty,' Angelina went on briskly. 'We don't cater for meals in the rooms here, I'm afraid. I've booked your free tour for tomorrow, starting at nine. Best to do it early in the summer before it gets too hot. Your guide will be waiting for you at five to nine at the cellar door, which is not far from the restaurant. Just follow the signs. I think that's all I have to tell you but please, feel free to ring and ask if you have any problems at all.'

'Oh, I'm sure we won't,' the wife beamed. 'This is all just so lovely.'

'Come on, kids,' the father said to his son and daughter, who looked about eight and ten respectively. 'Let's go and find our cossies. That pool sure looks good after our long drive. Thanks, miss.'

'Angelina,' she told him, pointing to her name tag.

'Angelina. Pretty name.'

'Pretty girl,' the wife said, but without a trace of spite, or jealousy. Angelina decided she liked her very much.

'OK, kids. Back into the car.'

Angelina had tried to keep her cool during the five minutes it had taken to go through her resort spiel. But all the time, she'd been watching Jake out of the corner of her eye.

No sooner had the navy sedan moved off than he

was out of the car and striding towards the reception room.

Angelina's gaze raked over him admiringly as he approached. It was the first time she had seen him in a suit, and my, he did look well in one. He looked well in any clothes, she conceded. And even better in nothing.

Angelina groaned and dropped her own eyes to the desk. She'd accused Jake of having a one-track mind last Sunday, but she was no better where he was concerned. One glimpse, and she was aching to rip his clothes off.

The small bell on the door tinkled as he pushed it open, Angelina pretending not to have noticed his arrival till that moment.

'Jake!' she said on looking up. 'Goodness, what are you doing here?'

He eyed her quite coldly.

'Cut the crap, Angelina. You saw me drive up. I know you did. I suggest you get someone else to take over here,' he commanded in a peremptory fashion. 'We need to talk.'

Angelina felt as if he'd punched her in the stomach. What was going on here? And who did he think he was, talking to her like that?

'I...I can't,' she replied, flustered by his rudeness. There *is* no one else. Not till five.' Barbara would take over at five for the night shift.

They both glanced at their watches. Five o'clock was fourteen minutes away.

'Is your place open?' he asked abruptly. 'I'll wait for you in there.'

Angelina hesitated to let him go into her home by himself. He might start looking around.

Though why would he...unless he'd found out something...?

The arrival of another car outside Reception forced her to make up her mind.

'Yes, it's open. Go on round and I'll be with you shortly. But what is this all about, Jake? You seem upset.'

'Upset,' he repeated, as though considering the word. 'No, I'm not upset. I'm bloody furious!' With that, he marched out, leaving Angelina to stare after him.

Has he found out about Alex? came the immediate question. But if so, how so? Had Arnold let something slip in his negotiations with Dorothy?

Angelina knew that the sale of Arnold's property was going ahead at a great rate. Money had been no object and Dorothy had had her lawyers rush through the searches. Contracts were being exchanged next week and she was going to move in a fortnight later.

Fortunately, Barbara arrived ten minutes early for work, Angelina relieved to let her take over so that she could bolt round and see what Jake wanted. Unfortunately, even in that short space of time, her nervous tension had reached dangerous proportions.

She hurried in to find Jake in her kitchen, making himself some coffee and looking as if he'd lost his case this week, instead of winning it.

'I'm here,' she said, unnecessarily, since she was standing in the same room, not ten feet from him.

His head turned and those icy blue eyes of his cut through her like knives.

'How long,' he ground out, 'did you intend to keep our son a secret from me?'

Angelina sagged against the kitchen sink. He knew.

'How…how did you find out?' she choked out, then slowly shook her head. 'Arnold, I suppose. He must have let it slip to Dorothy.' Alex was right. Arnold could be a bit of an old fool.

'Alex told me himself, in my office, just over four hours ago.'

Angelina gaped at him. This she had *not* expected. Oh, Alex…

'Naturally, when I was first told I had a visitor named Alex,' Jake ground out, 'I assumed he was your ex-lover. Imagine my surprise when I encountered a schoolboy. But I won't go into that, or even try to understand your sick reasons for letting me think such a thing. I am here because of the real person, the real Alex. Our son. Seems he saw me on TV last night and realised that I was the Jake Winters his mother had said was his father. No doubt because we look exactly like each other!'

Angelina groaned. So that was what had precipitated their son's actions. If only she'd thought of something like this happening. She herself had seen Jake on the news. What an idiot she was! But, of course, her mind had been on other things since last weekend. Her son had ceased to be her top priority for once.

Her remorse was acute.

But once she saw Jake's body language, the mother tiger in her came back with a vengeance. 'If you acted like this with him, Jake,' she bit out, her eyes narrowing, 'I won't ever forgive you.'

Jake's nostrils flared. 'Do you honestly think, after what *I* went through as a child, that I would do anything remotely hurtful to *my* son?'

Angelina was taken aback by the possessiveness in his voice. And the sheer emotional power.

This was not a man who was repulsed by the discovery that he was a father. Sure, he was shocked. And yes, he was angry. But only with her.

She smiled. She couldn't help it. 'He's wonderful, isn't he?'

'Bloody hell, Angelina, how can you smile at me after what you've done? Look, I understand why you didn't tell me about Alex when he was born, and during the years since. Aside from your father's natural hostility towards me, why would you? If I'd been in your boots I wouldn't have told me, either. But after we ran into each other again the way we did and you saw that I wasn't some kind of deadbeat, you should have told me then. Why, in God's name, didn't you? Especially when Alex was already pestering you to find me. Oh, yes, he told me all about that. Not one to hold back, is Alex. Unlike his mother,' Jake bit out.

Angelina remained guiltily silent.

'I asked you a question, Angelina. I expect an answer. Why didn't you tell me on that first Saturday? You had every opportunity, especially when I came back a second time.'

'I guess I was afraid to.'

'Afraid! Afraid of what?'

'Of your not wanting Alex!' she burst forth. 'You said you didn't ever want children.'

'Alex is a *fait accompli*,' he muttered. 'That's a different matter entirely.'

Angelina winced. He was right. She should have told him. 'You…you didn't tell him about us, did you?' she asked plaintively.

'What do you take me for, a complete fool? No, of course I didn't tell him about us. You have nothing to worry about. I made all the right noises. Did a better imitation of a father thrilled to discover he had a fifteen-year-old son than you'd see in a Hollywood movie. I also told him that I would come up and see you personally and smooth things over. He was worried sick how you would react when you found out he'd looked me up, since you had a deal to wait till Easter. Though might I add he seemed chuffed to find out I wasn't the jailbird you'd told him I was sure to be. He said he told you I wouldn't be, but you didn't seem to have the same blind faith in my character.'

She flushed, but lifted her chin defiantly. 'You have to appreciate it was a one-in-a-million chance that you'd turn out to be any good.'

'I'm not blaming you for that judgement call. You

did exactly what I would have done in your position. I suppose I could even forgive you for not telling me about Alex straight away. What I find *un*forgivable is that you didn't tell me the truth by the end of last weekend. What could you possibly have been afraid of by then?'

'Well, I...I...' How could she tell him that she was afraid he'd stop wanting to make love to her? It sounded so...selfish.

His sudden paling had her panicking.

He's guessed the truth. And he's totally appalled.

'It was that incident with the kid, wasn't it?' he said, startling her. 'And my telling you about my childhood. That's why you went all quiet on me. You were worried I might hit Alex like my mother hit me.'

'No! No, nothing like that at all! I'm sure you wouldn't do any such thing!'

'What, then?'

There was nothing for it now but to tell him the truth. In a fashion. 'I...I wanted to tell you. Really, I did. But I was afraid that it would change things between us. I thought...' She bit her lip and tried to find the right words.

'What did you think?'

'All kinds of things. At first, when I agreed to have lunch with you, I just wanted to find out what you were like, what kind of man you were, *before* I told you about Alex. You have to appreciate it was a terrible shock to me, Jake, when you turned up in my life, *and* when I found myself as attracted to you as

I was when I was just a girl. I thought I could control how I felt about you. But of course, I couldn't. Then, when the sex was so fabulous between us, I didn't want it to end. I wanted you to keep looking at me the same way. And making love to me. It was selfish of me, I know, but I…I've never felt anything like I do when I'm with you.' Tears pricked at her eyes. 'I'm sorry, Jake. Truly. I didn't mean to hurt you.'

'Well, I am hurt, Angelina. Do you have any idea what it was like, finding out we had a fifteen-year-old son like that?'

'I'm sure it was a shock.'

'That's an understatement.'

'I…I don't know what to say.'

'There's nothing you can say. The damage has been done.'

Angelina's heart sank. But then defiance kicked in. And resentment. Had what she'd done been that wicked, or seriously unforgivable?

Hardly.

'Well, I happen to think there is a lot I can say,' she threw at him. 'I've stood here, like a typically pathetic female, humbly listening to your poor-little-me tale. I've even been feeling sorry for you. But you know what? I think I'm all sorried out. Where is your sympathy for me? Do you have any idea what *my* life has been like? How hard it's been for *me*?'

'I have some idea. Alex told me. In fact, he told me more about you in the two hours I spent with him today than you have in two weeks. I know the sacrifices you've made for him. I know you've been a good mother. I know you never laid a hand on him, no matter how naughty he was. I know he thinks the world of you. I also know you don't date. *Ever.*' He glowered at her. 'It seems you've become a master at deception in a lot of things.'

'What do you mean?'

'You keep secrets from *everyone*, not just me. *I* know you've had lovers. You told me so. Yet your teenage son says there's never been another man in your life after me. He thinks you're a cross between the Virgin Mary and Mother Teresa. He even has this romantic idea that when you and I meet up again this time, we'll fall in love once more and get married.'

'Oh…' It wasn't so far removed from the romantic notions she'd been stupidly harbouring this last week.

'Yes, *oh*,' Jake said drily. 'Our son has to receive a reward for optimism, doesn't he?'

'He certainly does, considering who his father is. But for your information, Mr Smarty Pants, I have not had lovers. And I never said I had. You just jumped to that conclusion, probably because you couldn't conceive of anyone choosing to lead a celibate lifestyle. Which I did. For our son's sake. Don't think I didn't have offers. I've had plenty. So Alex was right. There's only been the one man in my life. *You!*'

Now that she'd blurted out the whole truth, Angelina rather enjoyed the shocked look on Jake's face.

'You can't seriously expect me to believe you haven't had sex in sixteen years?'

'No, I wouldn't expect you to believe that. Not *you*, a man who has a different girlfriend every other month and who can't even roll over in bed without reaching for another condom. But perhaps if you think about it a little more, you'll see I'm telling the truth. Why do you think I couldn't get enough last weekend? Because I was so frustrated, that's why.'

Jake stared at her. 'Frustrated.'

'Yes. Frustrated!' Her hands found her hips. 'I deserved a break after being such a goody-two-shoes for so long, don't you think? I could do with a few more, too. But I guess that's out of the question now. I always knew that as soon as you found out about Alex, everything would change between us. I'm no longer lover material, I'm the mother of your child. The *single* mother of your child. And, as such, to be treated with suspicion. It wouldn't take a genius to know that the invitation to come to your place this weekend is off.'

He looked stunned. 'Well, I…I need some time to think.'

Her smile was laced with bitterness. 'How come I'm not surprised? You can run but you can't hide, Jake. Alex has found you now, and if I know my son he won't let go. You're his father. Get used to it.'

'It's only been half a day, Angelina. Give *me* a break, will you?'

She laughed. 'You were right. You are going to be a pretty rotten father. Oh, I don't doubt you'll give lip-service to the role, but you just don't have what it takes in here…' She patted her hand over her heart, that heart which was breaking inside.

But be damned if she was going to show it.

'Alex's inter-school swimming carnival is on this Saturday,' she announced. 'It starts at one. Can I tell him you'll be there when I call him tonight? Or do you want time to think about that too?'

'I've already told him I'll be there.'

'No kidding. You've surprised me.'

'I surprised myself,' he muttered. 'Look, I'm doing my best, all right? I don't really know the boy. And I see now that I don't really know you.'

'Men like you never know anyone, except themselves.'

'That's a bit harsh.'

'Is it? I suggest you go home and have a good look in the mirror, Jake. If you can see past the shiny, successful, sexy surface, you just might not like what you find.'

'Angelina, I—'

'Oh, just go,' she snapped, and, wrapping her arms around herself, she whirled away from him to stare steadfastly out of the kitchen window.

She felt him staring at her. Felt his hesitation. But then he started walking. 'See you on Saturday,' he muttered, leaving his coffee untouched behind him on the counter.

By the time Angelina heard the Ferrari growl into life, she was crying her eyes out.

CHAPTER THIRTEEN

'I STILL find it hard to believe,' Dorothy said during dessert.

Jake, who always lost his appetite when he was stressed, or distressed, put down his dessert fork, his slice of lemon meringue pie still intact. 'You and me both,' he said with a weary sigh. 'I didn't sleep much last night. I kept seeing Alex's face when he called me Dad. He made me feel like such a fraud. I'm no hero, Dorothy. I'm just a man.'

'You're not *just* a man, Jake. You're an exceptional man. And you'll make an exceptional father.'

'How can you say that, knowing where I came from?'

'Because I know you. There's not a violent or a mean bone in your body. Angelina more or less said the same thing.'

'Angelina! Don't talk to me about Angelina!'

'Why? Because you're in love with her?'

Jake stiffened in his chair. 'I am not in love with her. I don't fall in love with liars.'

'She explained why she lied. And I, for one, understand her reasoning perfectly. So would you, if your male ego wasn't involved. She's a mother first and foremost. She was protecting her child.'

'She deceived me.'

'For the best of reasons. She wanted to get to know you first.'

'Yeah. In the biblical sense.'

'Oh, for pity's sake, will you get off your high horse? The girl obviously fancies you like crazy. She always did. You pack a powerful physical punch, Jake. She's a healthy young woman whose hormones have never had a chance. I don't blame her one bit if she wanted you.'

'Dorothy!'

'Goodness me, who do you think you're talking to here? A nun? I'll have you know I know exactly how Angelina must have felt last weekend. I was forty years old when I met Edward. OK, so I wasn't a virgin but as good as. I went to bed with Edward the very first night and we didn't sleep a wink. *All* night. Damn, but it was good.'

Jake just stared. He would never understand women. They could look so soft and malleable on the surface, when all the while, inside, they were tough as teak. And so damned surprising.

He hadn't expected Angelina to stand up to him the way she had yesterday. He'd expected her to wilt under his anger and beg his forgiveness. Instead, she'd read him the Riot Act and given him his walking papers.

She obviously didn't fancy him that much. *And* she sure as hell hadn't fallen in love with him last weekend as he'd foolishly hoped she had.

His goal to marry her now seemed even further away than ever. Perverse, considering they shared a child. Which brought him to the problem of Alex. Not that Alex was a problem child. He wasn't. He was a credit to Angelina. *He* was the problem. The father. The pathetic and panic-stricken parent.

He didn't know what to do or what to feel.

'Just go to the swimming carnival, Jake,' Dorothy advised, 'and let nature take its course.'

Jake shook his head. That was another thing about women. They were mind-readers. And weirdly perceptive. Look at how Sally had known Alex was his son at a glance. And then there was her knowing he was thinking of starting up his own business. How had she guessed that? Maybe the whole sex was in league with the devil.

'Stop thinking about yourself and *your* feelings,' Dorothy said sternly. 'Think about Angelina for a change. And what *she's* been through. Much more of a challenge than anything you've ever faced. Being solely responsible for looking after and bringing up a child is a massive job. She might have had her father for support but I doubt he was such a great help with the day-to-day problems of child-rearing. She did it all by herself, Jake. And she did a wonderful job by the sounds of things. The reason you've fallen in love with her is not just because she's physically beautiful. You've had oodles of good-looking girls before. It's because she's a beautiful person, with character and spirit. And you know what? I think she loves you for the same reasons.'

'Yeah, right,' he said drily.

Jake winced when Dorothy gave him one of the

savage looks she used to give him when he'd first come to live with her. 'I never took you for a coward, Jake Winters, but you're beginning to sound and act like one. You *do* love Angelina. And you love your son, even if you don't know him yet. Because he's your flesh and blood. And he loves you for the same reason. The three of you should be together, as a family. The reason Angelina got so stroppy with you yesterday is because that's what she wants too and she's afraid it's not going to happen. She's afraid her son is going to be hurt. She's afraid *she's* going to be hurt.'

'Have you finished?' Jake said ruefully.

'For tonight,' Dorothy returned as she stabbed her piece of pie with her dessert fork. 'There might be another instalment at some time in the future.'

'God forbid. Did Edward know you were like this?'

'Of course. Admittedly, he hated it when I was always right.'

Jake laughed. '*I* hate it too.'

Dorothy's breath caught. And then she let it out very slowly. He did love Angelina. Thank goodness.

'So what are you going to do about it?' she asked, feigning a composure she was far from feeling.

'Back off, Dorothy. This coward is still a male animal and likes to do things his way.'

'I don't really think you're a coward.'

'I know,' Jake said more softly.

'Er—do you think I could come to the swimming

carnival with you tomorrow?' Dorothy asked. 'I would dearly love to see the boy.'

'Only if you promise not to interfere.'

'Would I do that?'

'Yes. Now promise.'

Dorothy sighed. 'I promise.'

'OK,' he agreed, and Dorothy beamed.

She rose and scooped up Jake's untouched dessert. 'Coffee?'

'Mmm. Yes, please,' he said, watching blankly as Dorothy left the room. He was wondering what Angelina was doing and if she really might love him, as Dorothy said.

'I hate him,' Angelina muttered as she slammed the plates into the dishwasher.

'Hey, watch it with the crockery there, boss!'

'Let her break a plate or two, Kevin,' Wilomena advised from where she was scraping the remains of tonight's meals into the bin. 'Better than her breaking them over a certain person's head. Besides, they're her plates. She can do with them whatever she damned well pleases.'

'True,' Angelina growled, and slammed a few more in.

None of them broke. But then, they weren't as easily broken as other things. Like her heart.

'The bastard,' she grumped. 'How dare he say he had to *pretend* to be nice to Alex? As if anyone ever has to pretend to be nice to Alex.'

'Geez, Angelina!' Kevin exclaimed. 'Give the man a break.'

'That's exactly what she'd like to do,' Wilomena said drily. 'Across that stupid skull of his.'

'You women expect too much of a guy.'

'No kidding!' both women chorused.

'He'll come round. Just give him time.'

'Like, how long? A lifetime?' Wilomena said waspishly. 'That's how long it takes for some men to come to the party. If ever.'

'I think he sounds like an OK guy. He's going to Alex's swimming carnival tomorrow, isn't he?'

'Big deal,' Angelina muttered.

'Yeah, big deal,' Wilomena echoed.

'Women!' Kevin huffed. 'Impossible to please.'

'He could please her all right,' Wilomena said after Angelina had gone home and she and Kevin were stacking away the last of the things. 'He could tell her he loves her for starters, then ask her to marry him.'

Kevin laughed. 'You think that would please her? You know what she'd do? She'd throw back at him that he didn't really love her and he was only marrying her for the kid's sake. And then she'd say no, like a typical female.'

'Rubbish! She would not! Not if she loved him. And she does. Trust me on that. Women who love guys don't say no to a proposal of marriage.'

'You know, I'm glad to hear you say that,' Kevin said, and, drawing a small velvet box out of his white coat's pocket, he dropped to one knee then flipped it open. The cluster of diamonds in the ring glittered like his eyes.

'Wilomena Jenkins,' he said, 'I love you and I want you to be my wife. Will you marry me?'

Wilomena didn't say no. She didn't say a single word. She was too busy crying.

CHAPTER FOURTEEN

ALEX stood behind the starting blocks with the rest of his relay team, nerves making him shift from foot to foot. He swung his arms in circles to keep his muscles warm, and tried to focus on the race ahead, deliberately keeping his eyes away from the stand where he knew his parents were sitting together watching him, along with the old duck they'd brought with them.

'Dorothy's an old friend of mine,' his dad had introduced her before the meet began.

Old was right. And brother, had she stared at him.

Of course, that was because he looked so much like his dad.

His dad.

Alex scooped in a deep breath and let it out very slowly. It was still almost too good to be true, finding his father like that. He'd been confident that his dad would not be in jail. But he'd never dreamt he'd be a top lawyer. How cool was that? And what about that simply awesome car he drove? The guys at school had been green with envy when he'd rocked up on Thursday in a yellow Ferrari.

He'd felt so proud, introducing his dad around to his friends and teachers. He must have gone to sleep that night with a permanent smile on his face.

Now today was his chance to make his dad proud of him. Alex knew he wasn't good enough at his school work to line up for too many academic prizes. But he was his school's best swimmer. He'd already won the hundred-metre sprint. And the two hundred. Now he was lining up for the four-by-one relay, the last race of this meet, and he was swimming the anchor leg.

Kings were in front on the scoreboard. But only by a couple of points. If St Francis's could win this relay, the cup would be theirs. The trouble was, their second-best hundred-metre swimmer had come down with a virus that morning and they'd had to bring in the first reserve, who was three seconds slower. On paper, they couldn't possibly win, not unless they all swam above themselves.

Alex wanted to win. He wanted to win so badly.

They were being called up for the start. Alex felt sick. As team captain, he'd made the decision to put their slowest swimmer first, employing the tactic that sometimes a swimmer could swim a personal best if they were chasing. Of course, sometimes the chase theory didn't work. The behind swimmer tried too hard on the first lap and went lactic in the second.

The gun went off and their first and slowest swimmer was in the water, doing his best but possibly trying *too* hard. After he'd come in to the changeover several lengths behind, Alex wished he'd made the decision to go first himself. But he soothed his panic with the knowledge that Kings had sent their second-best swimmer off first.

By the second changeover, they'd caught up a couple of lengths. But then disaster happened. Their third swimmer's foot slipped on the starting block at the changeover, losing them another precious length. By the time he turned to come down for the second lap, he was trailing the Kings boy by a good five lengths. He dug deep, however, and came towards the wall only three lengths behind.

But even as Alex readied himself for the changeover, logic told him that three lengths were still too much. Sure, he'd won the hundred-metre race earlier in the afternoon. But only by a length. How could he possibly find another two lengths?

And then the voice came to him, across the pool, loud and clear.

'Go for it, son!'

He went, with wings on his feet, making up half a length in the changeover dive alone, coming up with the Kings swimmer's feet in his sights. There was no holding back. He wasn't close enough for fancy tactics, like riding in the other boy's wash. He put his foot down, his big arms slicing through the water, his even bigger feet churning with a six-beat kick right from the start.

You have to nail the turn, he lectured himself as the wall loomed into view. His lungs were bursting. He'd forgotten to breathe. No time now. He would breathe later, after he'd turned. He tumbled. His feet hit the wall and he was surging forward under the water. Up he eventually came, gasping for air but still swimming like a madman. He had no idea where the Kings boy was now. His head was turned the other way. All he could do was go like the hammers of hell.

His arms were burning. So were his legs. He'd never known such pain. Or such determination. He was going to win, not just for his dad, but also for his mum. He wanted to make her proud as well. Alex knew she'd given up a lot for him, and he wanted her to see that it had been worth it.

Not far now. He could hear the screaming. It had to be close. Just a bit more, Alex. You can do it. Stroke harder. Kick faster. The wall was coming up. Time it right. Dip down, stretch those fingers. You've got your dad's big hands. They have to be good for something.

He touched then exploded upwards, out of the water. He looked up, towards his mother. She had her hands over her face and she looked as if she was crying. His heart sank. He'd lost. He'd given it his all and he'd lost. But then the boy in the next lane was tapping him on the shoulder and congratulating him.

He looked up again. His mum was now wrapped in his dad's arms and the old duck next to them was grinning like a Cheshire cat, with her hand held up towards Alex in a victory sign.

Alex grinned back at her, his own hand punching up high into the air as he yelled, 'Go for it, Dad!'

CHAPTER FIFTEEN

'Is it always like that?'

Angelina lifted her head at Jake's question. They were back at his apartment, Angelina having driven there at Jake's request after the swimming carnival was over. She was sitting on the sleek red leather sofa once more, with a Malibu and Coke cradled in her hands, wondering when she could possibly get up and leave. Just being in this place with Jake, alone, was killing her. She'd thought she hated him this past week but of course she didn't. She loved him.

'Always like what?' she asked, her voice sounding as dead and drained as she was feeling.

'When your kid does something great. Does it always feel like that?'

'Like what, exactly?'

'Like your heart is going to burst out of your chest. Like you're on top of the world, a world bathed in everlasting sunshine.'

Angelina's own heart squeezed tight as all the fears which had been gathering that afternoon suddenly crystallised into one big fear.

'Yes,' she said flatly. 'Yes, it always feels like that.'

Jake sat down on an adjacent armchair with his

own drink in his hands. Scotch on ice, by the look of it.

'We have to talk,' he said, his tone serious.

'About what?' Angelina took a sip of her drink.

'You. Me. Alex.'

'Let's just stick to Alex.'

'I think we should start with you and me. After all, that's where Alex started, sixteen years ago.'

'A lot of water has gone under the bridge since then, Jake.'

'Yes. It certainly has. We're different people now, you and me.'

'One of us is, anyway,' she bit out, then took another sip.

Jake gritted his teeth. She wasn't making things easy for him. When she'd cried back at the swimming carnival and he'd taken her into his arms, he'd thought that everything was going to be all right. Alex had clearly thought so, too. *And* Dorothy. But the moment they were alone together again, she'd withdrawn inside a cold, hard little shell that he just couldn't penetrate.

Jake decided that a change of tactics was called for.

'So you're going to do it again, are you?' he said sharply.

That got her attention. 'Do what?'

'Lie to me.'

'I never lied to you,' she said defensively.

'Yes, you did. By omission. And by implication. Now you're doing it again.'

'I don't know what you mean.'

'You're pretending you don't care about me. That you don't love me.'

He watched her mouth drop open; watched the truth flash into her eyes.

'You *do* love me,' he ground out, his voice thick with emotion.

'I...I...' She shook her head from side to side, clearly unable to speak the words.

'You love me and you're going to marry me.'

'*Marry* you!' She jumped to her feet, her drink sloshing all over the rug. 'I am not going to marry you. When and if I marry, it will be to a man who loves me as much as I love him. And *not* because he covets my son. Oh, yes, I saw the way you looked at Alex today, Jake Winters, and I knew. I knew in my heart that you wanted my boy, not just for a weekend here and there but all the time. That was why I was crying so much.'

Jake snatched the glass out of her shaking hands and rammed it down on a nearby table along with his own drink before glowering at her with fury in his eyes and frustration in his heart.

'I've heard enough of this rubbish!' he roared. 'I *do* love you, woman. I probably love you even more than you love me! If you don't believe me, then come here...' Grabbing her hand, he dragged her with him into the bedroom, where he yanked open the top drawer of his bedside chest.

'I don't think that showing me how many con-doms you've bought is proof of love,' she said scathingly as she tried to tug her hand out of his. But he refused to let it go.

His producing a ring box and flipping it open to show a spectacular diamond engagement ring shut her up. But not for long.

'Good try, Jake. Good move, too. I've got to hand it to you. You're clever.'

Jake dropped the ring box on the bed, grabbed a piece of paper from the drawer and shoved it into her hands. 'That's the sales receipt. Care to check the date?'

Angelina's eyes dropped to the date. Wednesday. He'd bought the ring on Wednesday.

She looked up, tears in her eyes. 'You bought this *before* Alex went to see you?'

Jake had to steel himself against his own rush of emotion. 'I wanted to tell you I loved you and wanted to marry you last weekend. But I was afraid of rushing you. I thought you needed time. I was prepared to give you all the time in the world. But then I walked past this jewellery-shop window and saw this ring and I just had to buy it for you. When I put it in this drawer, I told myself I didn't care how long I had to wait till you wore it, as long as you eventually did.'

'Oh…' More tears rushed in, spilling over.

He wiped them away with his fingers, then curved his hands over her shoulders. 'I love you, Angelina Mastroianni. And you love me. So I'm not going to give you any more time. We've already wasted sixteen years.' He reached to extract the diamond ring from the box and slipped it on her left hand. It fitted perfectly. 'We're going to be married. Not hurriedly. Magnificently. Next spring. In St Mary's Cathedral. But that's just a ceremony. From this moment on, you are my woman, and I am your man, exclusively, till death do us part.'

'Till death us do part,' she repeated dazedly.

'Now tell me you love me.'

'I love you.'

He sighed and drew her into his arms, his lips burrowing into her hair. 'I think you should show me how much.'

CHAPTER SIXTEEN

SEPTEMBER—the first month of spring down under—
was an iffy month for weather in Sydney. Often cold.
Often rainy. But occasionally brilliant.

St Mary's Cathedral had never looked better than
it did that September afternoon, bathed in sunshine,
the nearby gardens just beginning to blossom. But
nothing could match the splendour of the bride as
she carefully mounted the cathedral steps.

Her dress was white chiffon, with a draped bodice
and a long, flowing skirt that fell from straight under
her impressive bustline. Her dark hair was sleekly
up, with a diamanté tiara as decoration. Her veil was
very long and sheer. Her neck was bare, but delicate
diamond and pearl drops fell from her lobes.

She looked exquisite. She also looked nervous,
which enhanced that glorious air of innocence that
often clung to brides, even those who were secretly
five months pregnant.

'I never appreciated till now,' she said to
Wilomena, 'just how nerve-racking weddings are. If
I hadn't had your help today, I'd never have been
ready in time.'

'That's what bridesmaids are for,' Wilomena returned, busily fluffing out the bridal veil. 'I'll be re-

lying on you for the same help when Kevin and I tie the knot later in the year.'

Angelina smiled at the girl who had fast gone from employee to confidante to best friend. 'My pleasure. And might I say that burgundy colour really suits you, despite your doubts? The style, too.'

Wilomena's dress was chiffon as well, calf-length, with a low neckline, spaghetti straps and a long, flowing scarf that draped softly around her throat and hung down to the hem at the back

'Mmm. Yes. I'm forced to agree. Kevin said he can't wait to get it off me later tonight,' she whispered.

'Come on, Mum,' Alex said, and took his mother's arm. 'Stop the girlie chit-chat. We don't want to keep Dad waiting too long. He was champing at the bit this morning.'

Angelina looked up at her son. So handsome he was in his tuxedo. And so grown up. He'd matured considerably since Jake had come into his life. The two of them spent as much time together as they possibly could, obviously trying to make up for lost time.

Angelina might have been jealous if both the men in her life hadn't been so happy. Besides, Jake still found plenty of time for her. Quality time. In bed and out.

The *Wedding March* started up, snapping Angelina out of her thoughts. Wilomena took her place in front of the bride and began the slow walk up the aisle, just as they had rehearsed. Angelina's arms tightened around her son's when her bouquet started to shake.

'Relax, Mum,' her son advised.

'How can you be so calm?' she cried.

'Well, there's nothing to be nervous about, is there? I mean…we all love each other here. Not only that, if I'm going to do Grandpa's job, I want to do it with dignity and panache, like he would have.'

Angelina's stomach tightened at the mention of her father. 'Do you think he'd mind my marrying Jake, Alex?'

'Grandpa? Nah. He'd be happy, I reckon. Especially now.'

'You mean because Jake's turned out to be such a good man?'

Alex stifled a laugh. 'Come on, Mum. This is me you're talking to. Because of the *baby*, of course! Dad told me all about it.'

'He *told* you!'

'Yeah, there are no secrets between Dad and me. He said it was all his fault, as usual.'

'Oh…'

'He also said if I ever get a girl pregnant this side of twenty-five, he's going to skin me alive,' Alex added with a grin. 'Hey, we'd better start walking. Wil's halfway up the aisle.'

They started walking, Angelina's head whirling. Jake had told Alex about the baby. And there she'd been, trying to hide her pregnancy, worried sick about what her son would think when he found out.

'You don't mind?' she whispered out of the corner of her mouth.

'Why should I mind? I always wanted a little sister.'

'You know it's a girl as well?'

'Yep. Dad's tickled pink.'

Which was true. Not that Jake had really cared if it was a boy or a girl. He just wanted them to have a baby together. He'd told her he wanted to experience fatherhood right from the start.

'Smile, Mum,' Alex ordered.

She smiled. And then she smiled some more. Alex was right. They all loved each other here. There was nothing to worry about.

Jake's heart lurched when she smiled. Then lurched some more when her smile broadened. God, how he loved that woman!

'What a babe,' Kevin muttered beside him.

'You can say that again,' Jake returned before he realised Kevin's eyes were on his fiancée across the way.

Those two only had eyes for each other. Jake knew that for a fact. Since quitting his job, he'd been spending a lot of time up at the winery, helping out there till he worked out what he was going to do, career-wise. Probably start up his own law practice. Sally had already indicated that she was for hire, at the right price.

He and Kevin had hit it off right from the start and when Angelina said she'd asked Wilomena to be her one and only bridesmaid, Jake had no hesitation in asking Kevin to be his best man.

'Angelina looks pretty good too,' Kevin added, and Jake laughed.

He caught Sally's eye in the third pew and gave her a wink. She winked back.

Then he smiled at Dorothy, who was looking just a little tense.

Dear Dorothy. *Smart* Dorothy as well. He would be forever grateful for the solution she'd come up with for a problem he had about names. The names of his children. He wanted both of them to have the same surname. *His*. But Alex was adamant about keeping Mastroianni as his surname and Jake could appreciate that. Still, with Dorothy's help, he'd sorted that all out. He hoped Angelina would be pleased, he thought as his gaze returned to his lovely bride.

Dorothy was determined not to cry during the ceremony, but she clutched a white lace-edged handkerchief in her hands, just in case. What a beautiful bride Angelina made. But what a handsome groom Jake was. Most touching of all was the way he was looking at the woman he loved as she came down the aisle. With so much tenderness. So much love.

Oh, Edward. You would have been so proud of him today.

But no prouder than she was. Maybe she wasn't his mother by blood, but she was in her heart. And

now there was a baby coming as well. A dear little
baby girl for her to help mind. And to love.

Oh, dear. She dabbed at her eyes.

Jake tensed when the priest got to the part which he
knew would come as a bit of a surprise to his bride.

'And do you, Jake Mastroianni, take…?'

Angelina reached out to touch the priest's arm.
'No, no,' she murmured. 'You've got it wrong. It's
Jake *Winters*.'

'Not any more,' Jake whispered to her. 'I had my
surname changed by deed poll. With Alex's approval, of course. I'm a Mastroianni now.' And he
glanced over his shoulder at his son, who nodded to
his mother with a wide smile.

'You've taken *my* name?' Angelina asked, looking
pleased, but stunned.

Jake sighed with relief. He'd done the right thing.
After all, he had no real attachment to his own name.
His poor mother had died some years back and he'd
never known any of his other relatives. But it was
rather ironic that he was to be called Mr Mastroianni
from now on.

I'll try not to discredit your name in any way,
came his silent promise to the proud Italian man who
had once broken his nose.

'Please go on,' Jake directed the priest.

The ceremony was a bit of a fog after that, Angelina
not surfacing till Jake lifted the veil from her face
and kissed her.

His lips on hers felt slightly different this time. Softer. More tender. More loving.

She looked up into her husband's eyes, those beautiful blue eyes that could look so hard at times. But not today. And certainly not at this moment. They were soft and wet with tears.

'Mrs Mastroianni,' he choked out, and she realised, perhaps for the first time, just how much he *did* love her.

'Mr Mastroianni,' she returned softly, and touched his cheek. 'My sweet darling. My only love.'

The world's bestselling romance series.

HARLEQUIN®
Presents

Seduction and Passion Guaranteed!

OUTBACK KNIGHTS
Marriage is their mission!

From bad boys—to powerful,
passionate protectors!

Three tycoons from the Outback
rescue their brides-to-be....

**Coming soon in Harlequin Presents:
Emma Darcy's exciting new trilogy**

Meet Ric, Mitch and Johnny—once three Outback bad
boys, now rich and powerful men. But these sexy city
tycoons must return to the Outback to face a new
challenge: claiming their women as their brides!

**MAY 2004: THE OUTBACK MARRIAGE RANSOM #2391
JULY 2004: THE OUTBACK WEDDING TAKEOVER #2403
NOVEMBER 2004: THE OUTBACK BRIDAL RESCUE #2427**

"Emma Darcy delivers a spicy love story...
a fiery conflict and a hot sensuality."
—*Romantic Times*

Available wherever Harlequin books are sold.

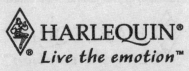

HARLEQUIN®
Live the emotion™

Visit us at www.eHarlequin.com

Harlequin Romance®

THE WEDDING PLANNERS

Where weddings are all in a day's work!

Have you ever wondered about the women behind the
scenes, the ones who make those special days happen, the
ones who help to create a memory built on love that lasts
forever—who, no matter how expert they are at helping
others, can't quite sort out their love lives for themselves?

Meet Tara, Skye and Riana—three sisters whose jobs consist
of arranging the most perfect and romantic weddings
imaginable—and read how they find themselves walking
down the aisle with their very own Mr. Right…!

**Don't miss the THE WEDDING PLANNERS trilogy
by Australian author Darcy Maguire:**

A Professional Engagement HR#3801
On sale June 2004 in Harlequin Romance®!

Plus:

The Best Man's Baby, HR#3805, on sale July 2004
A Convenient Groom, HR#3809, on sale August 2004

Available at your favorite retail outlet.

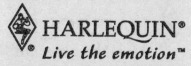

HARLEQUIN®
Live the emotion™

Visit us at www.eHarlequin.com

HRTWP

Beneath tropical skies, no woman can hide from danger or love in these two novels of steamy, suspenseful passion!

UNDERCOVER SUMMER

USA TODAY
bestselling author

ANNE STUART

BOBBY HUTCHINSON

Two page-turning novels in which romance heats up the lives of two women, who each find romance with a sexy, mysterious undercover agent.

Coming to a bookstore near you in June 2004.

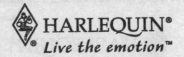

HARLEQUIN®
Live the emotion™

Visit us at www.eHarlequin.com

BR2US

"Joanna Wayne weaves together a romance and suspense
with pulse-pounding results!"
—*New York Times* bestselling author Tess Gerritsen

National bestselling author

JOANNA WAYNE

Alligator Moon

Determined to find his brother's killer, John Robicheaux finds
himself entangled with investigative reporter Callie Havelin.
Together they must shadow the sinister killer slithering in the
murky waters—before they are consumed by the darkness....

A riveting tale that shouldn't be missed!

Coming in June 2004.

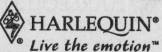

HARLEQUIN®
® *Live the emotion*™

Visit us at www.eHarlequin.com

PHAM

If you enjoyed what you just read,
then we've got an offer you can't resist!

Take 2 bestselling
love stories FREE!
Plus get a FREE surprise gift!

Clip this page and mail it to Harlequin Reader Service®

IN U.S.A.	IN CANADA
3010 Walden Ave.	P.O. Box 609
P.O. Box 1867	Fort Erie, Ontario
Buffalo, N.Y. 14240-1867	L2A 5X3

YES! Please send me 2 free Harlequin Presents® novels and my free surprise gift. After receiving them, if I don't wish to receive anymore, I can return the shipping statement marked cancel. If I don't cancel, I will receive 6 brand-new novels every month, before they're available in stores! In the U.S.A., bill me at the bargain price of $3.57 plus 25¢ shipping & handling per book and applicable sales tax, if any*. In Canada, bill me at the bargain price of $4.24 plus 25¢ shipping & handling per book and applicable taxes**. That's the complete price and a savings of at least 10% off the cover prices—what a great deal! I understand that accepting the 2 free books and gift places me under no obligation ever to buy any books. I can always return a shipment and cancel at any time. Even if I never buy another book from Harlequin, the 2 free books and gift are mine to keep forever.

106 HDN DNTZ
306 HDN DNT2

Name	(PLEASE PRINT)	
Address	Apt.#	
City	State/Prov.	Zip/Postal Code

* Terms and prices subject to change without notice. Sales tax applicable in N.Y.
** Canadian residents will be charged applicable provincial taxes and GST.
  All orders subject to approval. Offer limited to one per household and not valid to
  current Harlequin Presents® subscribers.
  ® are registered trademarks of Harlequin Enterprises Limited.

PRES02   ©2001 Harlequin Enterprises Limited

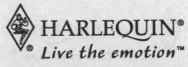

Forrester Square

LEGACIES . LIES . LOVE .

**Secrets and romance unfold at Forrester Square…
the elegant home of Seattle's most famous families
where mystery and passion are guaranteed!**

Coming in June…

BEST-LAID PLANS
by
DEBBI RAWLINS

Determined to find a new dad,
six-year-old Corey Fletcher
takes advantage of carpenter
Sean Everett's temporary
amnesia and tells Sean that
he's married to his mom,
Alana. Sean can't believe
he'd ever forget such an
amazing woman…but more
than anything, he wants
Corey to be right!

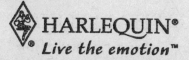

HARLEQUIN®

Live the emotion™